INTERNATIONAL HUMAN RIGHTS ART MOVEMENT

LITERARY MAGAZINE

2023 COLLECTED WORKS

Curated & edited by Bridget Reaume

A publication of the International Human Rights Art Movement (IHRAM)

INTERNATIONAL HUMAN RIGHTS ART MOVEMENT LITERARY MAGAZINE
2023 Collected Works

Copyright © 2024
International Human Rights Art Festival Inc., NY

All right reserved. No part of this publication may be reproduced, distributed, or transmitted in any form or by any means, including photocopying, recording, or other electronic or mechanical methods, without the prior written permission of the publisher, except in the case of brief qotations embodied in critical reviews and certain other noncompliance uses by copyright law.

For permission requests, contact Founding Producer Tom Block
and the IHRAM editorial team:
hello@humanrightsartmovement.org

Curated by IHRAM in the United States of America.
IHRAM, New York City, USA
www.humanrightsartmovement.org

Curated and edited by Bridget Reaume
Cover Design by Lisa Zammit
Cover Photo by Sandra Mayo

CONTENTS

Bridget Reaume
2 *Introduction*

Ewa Gerald Onyebuchi
4 *The Music of the Birds in Exile*

A. N. Grace
6 *The Dream Season*

Leila Zak
8 *Behind the Barbed Wire*

Olayioye Paul Bamidele
12 *Paradise of Poverty*

Brittany Dulski
14 *Regreso a Casa*

Nneamaka Onochie
16 *If Tomorrow Never Comes*

Eleanore Lee
20 *Milk*

Sharon Kennedy-Nolle
24 *Frisbee*

Lena Petrović
25 *Barcode Embargo*

Ruchikaa Bhuyan
26 *Hear Me*

Amina Akinola
28 *A Call for New Names*

Claire Joysmith
30 *¿Y Qué Hacer?*

TIMB Sara Augustine Laurence
32 *In Memory of Ekondo-Titi*

Kashvi Ramani
34 *11 Years Too Young*

Adesiyan Oluwapelumi
36 *Taxonomy of Identity*

CONTENTS

Sureswari Bagh (Translated by Pitambar Naik)
39 *The Lockdown Walk*

Susan L. Lin
40 *No Equa(ity)*

Goodwell Kaipa
41 *Merciless Mercenary*

Hec Lampert-Bates
42 *Plastic*

Heather Saluit
46 *Threshold*

Purabi Bhattacharya
47 *Cacti Left to Bloom*

Cyndy Muscatel
48 *Losing It*

Arina Alam
52 *Inverted Triangle Body*

Alyza Taguilaso
54 *Meditations in a Fractured Archipelago*

Tyler Hein
56 *Five Horses*

Sabahat Ali Wani
60 *A Familiar Sound*

Nwuguru Chidiebere Sullivan
66 *Eucharist I & II*

Adesina Ajala
69 *Hail & Brimstones in Sudan*

Mackenzie Duan
70 *Untouchability*

Uzomah Ugwu
74 *Purple Blouse*

CONTENTS

Basudev Sunani
75 *Mother Never Dies*

Uzomah Ugwu
76 *I Met America*

Arya F. Jenkins
77 *E. Palestine Ohio*

Dawn MacDonald
78 *Please Leave On*

Tania Chen
79 *When You Ask Me for Levity*

Tasneem Hossain
80 *A Mother's Oath*

Robert Pettus
82 *Kindergarden in Russia*

Ave Jeanne Ventresca
92 *Portrait in Watercolor: The Inhabitants of Houses*

Mira Mookerjee
94 *White Card*

Debasish Mishra
100 *An Orphaned Clothesline*

Joshua Effiong
101 *Self-portrait with Xylem*

Oliver Smith
102 *Before Windmill Hill*

DMT
104 *Red*

Nwuguru Chidiebere Sullivan
106 *Headless*

Meenakshi Bhatt
108 *Breaking Down*

Sam Safavi-Abbasi
110 *Snowflakes of Yesterday*

CONTENTS

Vyacheslav Konoval
111 *The World that Loved Executioners*

Nnadi Samuel
112 *Country of Bone and Midieval Rot*

Chinedu Gospel
115 *Boys of the Savanna*

Ananda Kumar
116 *Mr. Carter's Women*

Fadrian Adrian Bartley
122 *Skin Too Thick*

Chinecherem Enujoke
123 *Rippling Song of Scars*

Elaine Gao
124 *Simple Operations*

Ali Ashhar
125 *Amalgamation*

Kali Fox-Jirgl
126 *If Walls Could Talk*

Bhuwan Thapaliya
134 *Grandma*

Jade Wallace
136 *Lie Fallow*

Zaynab Iliyasu
146 *I Saw You*

Arathi Menon
147 *Manifesto of the Repressed*

Haro Istamboulian
148 *Free*

2023 IHRAM LITERARY MAGAZINE

INTRODUCTION

BRIDGET REAUME | EDITOR & CURATOR

This is a transcendent time. So we're told. As members of the 4.9 billion people actively engaging in the online social sphere, we are bombarded with world news, opinions, stories — bias, fact, and a muddled mess somewhere in between the two — every time we unlock our phones or open a new tab.

We know, however, that through conversation, reflection, and shared experiences, we become a more empathetic people. These values are ingrained in us from a young age. Our childhood storybooks and primary school teachers taught us the power of empathy; to listen to our peers' feelings and consider the needs of others in addition to our own needs. Then why, in an era of mass, consistent, global communication, are we more defensive, distrusting, and anxiety-riddled than ever before?

We are all, at our core, the same; traversing every new day, tending to invisble wounds new and old and simultaneously experiencing the beauty of life through interactions with our fellow people. As the International Human Rights Art Movement's Publishing Editor, I have the privilege to read the stories and personal reflections of writers from across the globe. Some are heartwarming, beautiful works of art, depicting the unyielding human ability for empathy and love. Others are shocking, shattering, and raw, showcasing a resilience through trauma I never thought possible.

Art is the window to the soul — *thank you, Lady Bird* — however, I'll argue that in the digital age, where we find ourselves stuck in a never-ending traffic jam of content, conflict, and contradicting conversations, art slices through the noise. A reminder of our *humanity*. No matter how we evolve, we are, and have always been, storytellers.

If art is a window, consider this magazine a direct line — a can and string mechanism — to a fellow human, a world away. The beauty of the International Human Rights Art Movement is that we are not just another soldier in the fight for global human equality; we are a peaceful space for human connection and reflection.

Writers, thank you for sharing your stories with us, and now, the world! Readers, thank you for joining the conversation. If you are ready to share your story, pick up that tin can and give us a shout.

Bridget Reaume
Publishing Editor
International Human Rights Art Movement
Edinburgh, UK
January, 2023

THE MUSIC OF BIRDS IN EXILE

EWA GERALD ONYEBUCHI | NIGERIA

mama is not dead.

she sits under the plum tree beside my window.

she's a bird with prominent feathers; she's a girl of fifteen

she's just like me—broken and beautiful

her eyes are armed with letters from the past:

darts of war and hunger splitting the bowel of cities in halves.

tonight, mama calls me by name: Nkonye.

the river in her voice drowns the ache in my chest. her face wears

the shimmer of the moon. in her eyes, a thousand shooting stars

spring with the weight of what they know—

deep yearnings yolked in baskets of time.

on her hand, I trace planets of fresh warmth,

memories pulsating with every intake of breath—

the first time I said mama with the guttural inclination of a child

from her body I drank the first sun and morphed into a garden of promises.\

mama's voice is a guitar strumming broken chords

the earth under our feet is a mouth humming

the wind drums the tale of bodies meshed in love and loss.

tonight, a trickle becomes a deluge

tonight, my body learns the music of birds in exile

she takes me through a door in her eyes and

we amble down a valley of bones—

a long line of women who gave up silence

to sing their loved ones to the afterlife

women who carried the world and their dreams in chapped palms

tonight, my mother teaches me how to carry my dreams—

in jars of wet clay she mends the rift on my

tongue and weaves a new language

A girl is a mirror to the world, she says. a fine mix of blood and water and fire.\

mama breathes into me and I become dough—

a pile of soft white batter she cracks open with her fingers.

I watch her knead me into several shapes—

versions of myself tucked in a box

versions I revel in.

she runs me through the furnace and I do not melt.

she says a girl must be both silk and rock to

survive the manliness of the sun.

it was dawn, and I rode into the sun with a smile.

THE DREAM SEASON

A. N. GRACE | ENGLAND

Last night I drank a litre of table wine;

that stuff that comes in a box.

Last night they released The Panama Papers.

Now—days months years later—

it's like no one remembers

and everyone is shouting he's behind you!

But I'm in quicksand

and nothing works like it should

and my legs won't move

and no one knows anything

and no one remembers anything.

They remember *Make America Great Again.*

They remember *Get Brexit Done.*

Hell

maybe they even remember *Keep Cool With Coolidge.*

At some point, I remember that litre of table wine

and I think maybe none of it ever happened at all.

NO ONE KNOWS
NO ONE REMEMBERS

THE DREAM SEASON
A. N. GRACE

BEHIND THE BARBED WIRE

LEILA ZAK | CHINA | YOUTH WRITER

Gaunt and hollow-eyed, they stared through the mesh: people who didn't look like people, enshrouded by a sickness that seemed to cling to the air. They were stick-thin, no more than skin and bone, and swimming in a scent so rancid I could taste it through the rain. Some stood hunched over with their hands on their knees, while others were keeled over on the ground, or leaning on one another for support. What each one of them shared, though, was the same hopeless acceptance staining the little life they had left in their eyes.

They were desensitized, more animal than human, trapped in a communal cage, and left to bathe in their own sick. They barely blinked as they looked up to receive my arrival, and through the lethargic mist of shock and fear, they looked hours—if not minutes—away from death.

Further back inside the enclosure, a group of four men were face-to-face with the ground, suspended above the wet earth by nothing other than their hands and toes. They were forced to do push-up after push-up, over and over again, at the mercy of none other than the two young soldiers standing in listless cruelty over them.

I watched in horror as one of them collapsed into the earth, endowed with relief for no more than a couple of seconds before pushing himself back into formation with terrified alacrity. As the soldiers began to swing their whips, I couldn't suppress my grimace. The man's back was made a battlefield as he was subjected to an endless series of whips and lashes that seemed to never stop coming. I wanted to cover my ears, to muffle the sound, but I was locked into place. I couldn't move.

The longer I looked, the more I felt like I was going to collapse, too. There was a woman with two hollow caverns, gaping depressions where her cheeks should have been, clinging to the steel brambles that divided her from the outside world. Desperation marred her trembling hands as the fence rattled weakly beneath her grip. Despair, so raw that I had to look twice, distorted her gaze as it met mine, eyes imploring, begging me to do something—anything—to get her out. As if I could.

It was only when the soldiers tired of swinging that the whipping from behind her drew to a pause. But even so, the men labored on, their muscles rippling in fearful compliance, enduring it all in a silence that described their pain louder than any curse, groan, or grimace could.

I COULDN'T BEAR TO WATCH IT ANY LONGER. I FORCED MYSELF TO TEAR MY GAZE AWAY, BUT WHEREVER I LOOKED, THERE WAS ONLY MORE SUFFERING.

It was a soldier's playground—a sandbox enclosed by guards and barbed wire where shovels and toys were replaced by whips, rifles, and machine guns.

As I stared at the pitiful creatures, stunned into stupefaction, I couldn't help but realize something—a nagging revelation that drew goosebumps to my skin: they didn't look like they were ethnically Burmese. And at that thought, a shudder of icy foreboding was sent rippling through me. They looked like Nadia, they looked like my brothers, and... well, they looked like me. It was then that an icy cocktail of dread and understanding flooded over me. I willed myself to shake my acquiescence away; I couldn't be indecisive—not now. I willed myself to run, but the fists shackling me into place were too tight.

Without taking even another moment to think, I conjured up the will and the breath to scream. I opened my mouth, my chest on fire, and let my voice split open the sky. Making use of the gloved hands holding me down as support, I drove my arms into theirs, and, suspended in mid-air, began to kick, batter, and thrash. Commotion ripped through the three soldiers and I, and in a flurry of arms, gloved hands, and weapon shafts, I wasted no time in ripping myself away from the paths of the flying hands hurtling toward me. They were trying to stop me in my tracks, but I wouldn't let that happen. I wouldn't freeze this time—not again.

And so, I took off, relying on chance alone to work in my favor. And, as if fate itself was at play, I managed to barrel straight into the soldier on my left as he fumbled to get me back under his grip. Panic drew a swarm of butterflies with burning wings into my chest, but even despite how it burned, I forced myself to extend my stride, propelling one leg after the other as far as each pace would take me. Flames were licking up my legs as I ran, but there was no way I was going to stop now.

They had started running too. The soldier I had crashed into swung his arms in a clumsy attempt to intercept my path, to which I had just managed to swerve out of the way. Sliding out of arm's reach, I heard yelling above the thunder thrumming through the sky, but it only gave me reason to run faster. The wind was liberating, rushing through my hair as I hared down the muddy path and into the brush. I caught a glimpse of Nadia as she waited for me, poised to pick up her pace as soon as I'd reached her ground, and the second I did, we took off together, not daring to look back.

I embraced the rain as my feet sunk into the muddy ground, offering brief footholds that stabilized me against the raging wind. The jungle, flying by us as we ran with the storm, was a swathe of green and brown, undergrowth and overgrowth, land and sky, as it soared with us at our sides. The wind, carrying the storm—and us, our lives—drove us on through the suffocating foliage, and as we neared a hollow that opened out into the plain ahead, the sinking feeling that had submerged itself within my chest finally seemed to lift. Until then I hadn't dared turn around. I couldn't bring myself to rip myself from the reverie of relief and exhilaration washing over me. Then I turned around, and the gunshots started blasting.

The sound of bullets being fired split the air in two, commanding silence through even the sickening clamor of the storm. My ears seemed to burst as blood roared inside of them, and each blast filled my mouth with the overwhelming reek of earth as it struck through bark and fern alike time and time again.

Run: that was the only thought raging through my mind.

Run faster, I urged. But at the same time, I was running out of breath. Breathe in, run, breathe out, repeat. The cycle was never-ending.

Dancing through the undergrowth and choking on the fear that rolled off of us in waves, it became an increasingly hopeless effort attempting to dodge the bullets hurtling past. I stiffened as one whizzed past my ear. Any closer, and it would have ripped right through me. I fought to breathe, but as much as I heaved, I could only take in so much air with every breath. It was no use; we were slowing down.

PARADISE OF POVERTY

OLAYIOYE PAUL BAMIDELE | NIGERIA

You can tell: the poplars, shredding their leaves.
Fruits, unstitching their stems to the floor.

Perhaps to seek freedom. In this paradise,
everyone—everything—wants to be alone,
independent. Here, I watch
families like shrapnels, shred

themselves. If lack of knowledge is the only reason
my people perish, then this world is a congress

of ruins; litanies, falling to ashes, where only
a few minutes it's flirting in glowing. I don't know
how to wax poetic: to say poverty crawls into the
city like lice into unwashed hairs, & chew

everything that stalks wealth. Moths on new white linen.
Look at it: the televised

image of our government, gobbling economic
resources. They open their mouths on
the dais and a cyclone belch out
lies, corruption and lusting flies.
I wonder — how long are we going to

continue inhaling their breath? How long
Will we allow them to spin us senseless,
filching even the wildflowers in our hands?

We are in the Paradise of Poverty, famine
transfiguring our Eden to deserts. Our hands

stiff from reaching the middle tree fruit. Our hands, tremble
from threatening words 'do not eat or you will die'; arrow at us.
Arrow at the candlelight, burning hope in the dark.

REGRESO A CASA

BRITTANY DULSKI | USA

Buenos Aires, Argentina (2006)

Ana bustled around her small senior living apartment downtown. It was a nervous kind of energy; the kind that requires a deep focus on something like removing non-existing scuff marks on the floor. She looked out the window for her ride to meet her son, for the umpteenth time. Her son Christian and his family would meet her at the plaza, near the president's house. They said they would. Christian's wife Beatriz was coming, which wasn't thrilling. It's not that Ana viewed Beatriz as la problema, but she thought he could have done much better. The person she most looked forward to seeing was Carlota, her granddaughter. She had only seen a couple of pictures of her, but she looked like a very young Christian.

A couple of women from her retirement community were tagging along to meet their kids. Ana didn't really want to lose her focus for this reunion, which was her and Christian, but she appreciated the company of other women. All of the women wore white scarves and hoped that their kids would recognize them in what was sure to be an extensive crowd. It was peak tourist season. Ana looked at the sign she carefully crafted last night making sure that every word was large enough for anybody in the city center to see. As they prepared to leave for the city center, Ana looked at her apartment, satisfied with its level of cleanliness and hoped that Christian would enjoy it as well. She also had made Carlota a couple of dresses that she hoped would still fit, babies outgrow clothes so fast. Beatriz would never approve of these gifts.

The walk from Ana's apartment to the plaza seemed infinite. The city was crowded with tourists as she expected. All of the women spoke not a word once they arrived at the spot where they told their kids to be and began to set up. Ana could see the president's mansion. She had been invited there a couple of times but always politely declined. It seemed pointless to meet the president without Christian. At 10:00 AM Ana opened her sign.

¿Dónde Están?

Christian Desaparecido 4 agosto 1979
Beatriz Desaparecido 4 agosto 1979
Carlota Desaparecido 4 Agosto 1979.

IF TOMORROW NEVER COMES

NNEAMAKA ONOCHIE | NIGERIA

She soaked me in a hot bath, strengthened my legs, and held down my thighs so that the hot water burned through my skin and inside my privates. I neither winced nor objected — I was used to the ritual of pain. It had left its trademark in my heart; its imprint in my soul. I let mama do what she knows best — make up for the nightmare of dusk which had become my reality. She used an iron sponge and scrubbed my back with ferocity. She scrubbed each breast like she scrubbed the mortar after pounding cassava to eradicate any remnants and wrung me like she did her kitchen rag. Flagrantly she spread my legs and scrubbed my privates for what seemed like ten minutes. She would scrub for a whole day if she could. She scrubbed away my sins; our sins.

"Did it hurt much?" She inquired and I nodded in affirmative. My everyday reality, excluding the days I welcomed my monthly flow. Like a bird out of its cage, I would have a flimsy savor of freedom 'till I become dry. Last night — like every other — he stalked into my room as I lay still on the bed, pretending to be fast asleep. His weight compressed the bed as he sat, stinking of beer and tobacco. He dipped his hand into my gown and squeezed my breast like an orange. His breath, fast and eager. He turned me over and unzipped his pants with one hand he tore my underwear and rummaged through me, moaning.

"Be a good girl and bear it all," mama's voice echoed in my ears. I kept my eyes squeezed shut until he left.

"I'm sorry," mama muttered after she was done bathing me. I didn't reply — she apologized the same, day after day. I wondered what she apologized for, maybe that she wasn't able to save me from her husband my stepfather or that she was always outside my door while he lavished me and run his bath afterward or that she willed the intricacies of our lives to the man who battered her.

"You are our salvation Olaedo." Those were Mama's words at night, as she combed my soft, kinky hair with a hot comb, rubbed flower-scented ointment on my body, appareled me in her red gown, and handed me a glass of a clear drink that burned through my throat. "All at once," she coerced. I threw the remains in my mouth and swallowed hard.

"MAMA WHY CAN'T WE LEAVE… WE NEED HIM."

"For what exactly. For the crumbs he brings home or the meager sums he gives you till my monthly visitor comes. He is foul-tempered and tight-fisted. I fumed.

"He is not that bad Olaedo, he shelters us, protects us and feeds us."

So much for the necessities of life, I wanted to say but instead I rolled my eyes and blinked away the tears lingering at the corner of my eyes. I wondered if she believed her own lies, the ones she had so intricately woven its fabrics and concealed every hole.

Mama had closed down her beer parlour, because her husband complained he detest the bile of lust in the eyes of men who stare at her buttocks and fucked her in their minds. He said he would open a suitable business for her, that compliments his status as a police officer. *He never did.*

Each time she reminded him, he would hit her. We had her head stitched in different clinics so the other doctors wouldn't ask us questions or raise a brow. He accused Mama of having the cacoethes for prostitution in the disguise of an apt for business. The day her requests stopped was one early harmattan morning. He had filed out a sharp-looking dagger, brandishing it on her face, daring her to say one more word on the matter.

I stood wobbly beside her, my heart in my mouth. Struck dumb with fear. Anxious bile boiling in the pit of my stomach. She looked at me, in my terror-filled eyes, and she dropped her gaze to the floor, wordlessly admitting submission.

"*Ashewo*" he muttered. Abruptly, he turned and walked out the door, slamming it behind him.

That night he stalked into my room and fitted his weight at the edge of my bed. He smelled of tobacco, suya, and onion. He raised my gown, and inserted a crooked finger inside my privates. He hung my legs on his shoulders, kneading my buttocks with his hands, and rode me like a maniac each thrust more painful than the other. Like always, I pretended to be dead. He finished with a scream his body jerking and he slumped on me. A few minutes later he rose and meandered out of my room.

***

I sat numb, in the boiling tub while Mama scrubbed me with her iron sponge. How do I tell mama that the pain she is trying to wash away wasn't in the swell of my breast or down my thighs? The pain nestled deep in my soul and fettered in my heart.

"Open your mouth," she whispered, pausing her work. I heeded. She placed two tablets in my mouth and handed me a glass of warm water. She continued, raising my legs and scrubbing the sole of my feet, vigorously at first, then gently, massaging my feet and strengthening each toe. I closed my eyes, and rested my head back as tears cascaded down my cheeks betraying my callous strength.

"Here." She placed a towel over my shoulders.

I wrapped my bosom and lumbered to my room, my feet leaving a trail of water droplets. I entered my room, closed my door securely, sat on my bed, and dipped my finger inside my privates where there the bright red blood trickled. My momentary freedom and the commencement of Mama's miseries.

I walked to the kitchen, and stood by the brown wooden door, my arms folded. I watched her dice onion in a stainless plate busy in her state yet aware of my presence.

"My visitor has come," I announced.

She paused, nodded, and continued dicing. We both understand the implications of my monthly flow. At dusk he snuck into my room like a thief in the night, fondled my breast, and inserted his hands into my privates, where he felt the tampon. He heaved, cursed, and kicked the foot of my bed, storming out of my room and slamming the door as he left. I opened my eyes and sat on the bed.

The bickering in their room echoed through the night. He threw things in anger. I heard Mama's sobs. At an unknown hour of the night, I tiptoed to their room, and peeked through the hole in the bedroom door. The room was poorly lit but I saw it nonetheless. He was raping Mama, his hands clutching her neck. I drug my feet back to my room and lay in my bed, my heart pounding heavily I thought it would tear through my chest.

I closed my eyes and prayed tomorrow never comes, eventually dozing off with Mama's sobs lurking in my dreams.

MILK

ELEANORE LEE | USA

I Roar of an ancient ocean drawn
And moved by the moon.
It was here first—
Before annual statements of profit and loss.
Before airports or truck stops or the increasingly significant
microchip industry,
A warm and secret sea whose
Scented and rhythmic
Heave and flow
Is
Beneath the thin skin of our ways.
Below pavement and parking lot.
Beneath the flesh.

They brought the child to her.
And for the first time
She saw
The pinched face
Whose slate gray eyes looked past her.
The baby smelled of chemicals and pain.
Slowly she unwound the cloths
And spread out skinny toes and fingers.
Bowed legs my little frog
She gave life and on the third day
The milk came in.
The crying is stilled and peace drops
Like a curtain.

II

                    Outside it grows dark and the streetlights
                                                          Light
                         Reflecting off wet sidewalks far below.

                    It is almost five and my breasts burst and drip.
                              (The baby is awake and waiting.)

                              The workplace hums and sighs
                            With ringing phones and soft voices.
                  Outside the rain streams soundlessly down the glass.

(I know your voice is raised now.
Gummy toothless squint-eyed bawler.
You can't even make tears yet.
What do you know?
Like children skull-eyed
In distant lands
How are you to know?
Like them,
You know what you need to live.)

My shirt's soaked through.
Trapped in this shaft of steel and stone and glass,
I watch the clock hand move
And wait to be with you.

Abraham,
Sparing his beloved son Isaac,
Sacrificed the ram.

There's nothing noble about the cow or goat.
Milk-givers,
How many epics were written of them, after all?
Basically clean, companions of man,
Kosher.
Loving of brambles and buttercups.
The goat aggressive in her way.
The cow diffident and slow.
Both capable of great stubbornness,
Neither having made a reputation inwar.
They figure in the Bible along with sheep and wives
As a sign of great richness.
Our fathers slaughtered goats to honor

First the gods,
Then God.
Spilled blood on the altar.

No man ever made a miracle of milk
Like water into wine or
Wine to blood.
(Like the blood that told me month by month
You had not yet come.)
Simple as human kindness,
No man has lived without it.

IV

I'm here
Small red and mottled burden
Damp hot and salty
Hair glued eyes squeezed tight shut
Mouth wide
Nuzzling and rooting
Rosebud mouth sweet breath
Milk blister
My fingers clumsy on the buttons.
Flesh on flesh
At last
The gigantic tug
And pull
Suction
Turns me inside out
Pulls me down that dark tunnel
Toward the
Surge and swell.
Rinsed by the warm tide,
Know my power.

FRISBEE

SHARON
KENNEDY-NOLLE
USA

TO FILL IN THE BLANK

Two weeks later, I visit.
Kneeling now on the mound,
my face so close
I can eat your dirt.

But what's this
opening, escaping,
leaking back?
giving way, a sinking
I could fall into,
following the stone-plumbed line,
willing to switch places?

Just air escaping,
earth-sighs,
normal, the undertaker says
after the ground thaws suddenly

But it goes deeper
the more I kneel, stones trickle farther, faster
down, so I have to
scoop furiously with whatever stone,
any slab I can grab,
avalanche after my hand, working
to fill in the blank.
With a Frisbee now (the only hard edge from the car)
scraping dirt over the O-gape

How you'd cackle and scorn me again,
my toy tools even while other clayey mouths open,
venting, asking for answers.

BARCODE: EMBARGO

LENA PETROVIĆ | SERBIA & USA

Your hands full of worthless cash. Borders are sealed, price tags lost in fire, supermarkets emptied offering pickles alone. No one studies the shelves or shops for fun. You're looking for the exit, ride to a bar. There is no traffic. Gas stations are run by the warlords. Boulevards smell of sulfur and distant explosions have you on high alert.

To manage your cravings, retail shelves are void. The line for milk starts with the sunrise. Early birds count zeroes on the banknotes. At eight in the morning, patience is out of stock, bread has gone underground. Your family starts worshiping the holy trinity — flour, water, and yeast — making a fritter miracle when nothing else sustains.

Extravagant foreign aid: a shop line turns into a street parade. Neighbors carry flour sacks like rugby balls. Grannies cuddle oil boxes like pups. Ladies seize sugar cubes like stolen diamonds. At the register, you plead guilty, living under an ugly, fearmongering ruler, and watching his pretty television. Beware of a hissing can!

Smugglers are your sole saviors. They exchange the paper money for Deutschmarks. Chocolate, salami, and jeans gleam in their car trunks, duty-free delis. As you chew an illegal snack, the embargo enlightens you: it is the lack of supply that creates the demand. At first, you are isolated and hungry, then ambitious and capable.

The solitary pickle jar whets aching appetite, stirs anger, propels unrest. As you taunt and boo on the main square, trying to reclaim your future, suicide rate increases, buddies disappear, leaders travel the world. At buffet tables, the heads talk ceasefire and export-import games. The most charming one toasts to their newest success story.

HEAR ME

RUCHIKAA BHUYAN | INDIA | YOUTH WRITER

So, they say —
if someone breaks into your home
you can call the cops and have a say over what's your own
but if someone breaks into my home
and thieves me of the life between my thighs
I am silenced?
and when I call upon the
system in place to support the people
I am robbed of my free will?

Hear me —
if you want to save lives
then let them be borne out of love
and not compulsion.
your chant of human rights is meaningless
if you establish shackles and name them
'rights'
coerce a burden on bodies unknown to you
and call it 'love'.

Hear me —
my mother loves me beyond measure.
she fights every day for my rights
in spite of her own.
but if I were born out of compulsion
forced on her, unwanted,
a product of sacrificial surrender
to manacles you confuse with morals
my mother would love me unconditionally still,
but I wouldn't ever be able to love myself
knowing her rights and autonomy
were robbed.

Hear me —
in saving one life you are ruining
two.

So, they say —
to tone it down.
why?
after all, we are generations apart,
and I'll scream as loudly as I must
till my words reach you in the past.

A CALL FOR NEW NAMES

AMINA AKINOLA | NIGERIA

My origin traces back to whispers.
Scattered rose brambles and buds that cannot share their stories.

Today, I watched a lightning bug fly out the belly of a flower.
Shaken from its confines rooted in cement.
I ask: how long do we starve before it drains our souls?

In my country, everyone hauls a casket in their shoulders,
waiting to waste away with the passing of days.
My casket is full of skeletons — of children — wasted from hunger.
Bone-dry hands that yearn for rain.
In this world, we are all hungry — craving a different dish,
like the lads lurking around the lane of Okokomaiko.

In Agege, the children lack their namesake bread.
Men don't cry, here — they stare blankly into the sky with no tears left to flow.
At the market today, a girl attempted to steal garri for eba her body was shoved
between hot grates barbecued. I ask again, who will account?

Who will fashion our future when our hands are fumbling to beat away the smoke?
Here poverty is a menace yet to be dismantled.
Here poverty has grown beyond the wings of charity, yet we can not clamp its cord.
Who will combat this chronic ailment that merges our nation to mortality?

I started yesterday by tucking some notes in a beggar's bowl,
I wished I could do more, but my pocket taunted and laughed at me.
How long do we plan to hem nairas in bowls?
When did our people's hunger become invaluable?

Allah ba mu sa'a — rhythm on our lips
Poverty — *e choke*
Sama us beta empowerment, with a platform to manifest change.
Not one that leaves us to wander, & wonder, when will our savior arrive

Hope is a thing that withers a man before his death.

No amount of given fish will quench a man's hunger
like the effect of hooks allotted to him to hunt.
man, I say: not fit to live off fish alone, e no fit

Give us the map to fair fates;
we yearn to rally our tongues — over a greener community;
we yearn— to bear new names.

¿Y QUÉ HACER?

CLAIRE JOYSMITH
MEXICO

The stars count them,
telling their stories.

A thousand and one nights
could not account for them

nor tell a thousand and one
Scheherezadian stories
for sheer survival.

¿Y QUÉ HACER?

The victim dies in agony
once
unravelling karmic knots.

¿Y QUÉ HACER?

The perpetrator dies
a thousand and one
times in deep ignorance:

his karma seared for
a thousand and one
years to come.

¿Y QUÉ HACER?

The family grieves, weeping,
a thousand and one times,
replicating sorrow,
perhaps hatred,
their karma suspended
between options.

¿Y QUÉ HACER?

How many nights of unabated rage
can be held in a single glass of water
and a sugarcoated sleeping pill?

¿Y QUÉ HACER?

Questions burst into life
as the relentless future
seeds in our now.

Who is to receive
multiple compassion?

2023 IHRAM LITERARY MAGAZINE

¿Y QUÉ HARÉ MOS?

IN MEMORY OF EKONDO-TITI

TIMB SARA AUGUSTINE LAURENCE | CAMEROON

A blackish dawn covered Ndian
Along National Highway 16, fierce tears wet to the bone.
A dying ray of sunlight tries to loosen their skeletal fingers, clenched under the
Frigid cold

Through the cloud of smoke, the city hobbles.
Men screech and birds fly away,
Hundreds of bewildered people run haggardly in this dark silence where cries
rise. Pain crumples their faces,
With a dead voice, they call to the sky that you just joined.
A horde of soldiers surround the place,
Their radios crackle and fade away.

In the distance, your remains slumber,
The ashes of your lives are scattered on the trail that leads to this room that you
did not want to leave.

Everything is gone!

The school is only a few corners walled with cinder blocks,
The windows are broken,
twigs and bits of hair fall in the trickle of blood.

Your families, adorned with the dark fabrics of the night, cry tirelessly.
Their tears stream down their faces which now contain a river of sorrow.

Their eyelids close on this nameless horror.
A vain color of sunshine and dreary looks illuminates a memory:
You wore school uniforms,
Laughing with hope at the promises of the future that your teachers proudly told you.

Forged of the golden and silver light of your dreams, you take the road little taken,
But *don't go gently into that good night*

Rage! Rage! Against your murderers.
In your new homes,
A procession of ghosts walks,
Their steps on the asphalt disturb for a few moments the silence of the dead

Still, a memory resounds:

Your names ring: *Jocelyne, Emmanuelle, Kum...*
Forced to walk the road meant for older men
And our eyelids close on the epitaph where are engraved some
notes of your short happiness

11 YEARS TOO YOUNG

KASHVI RAMANI | USA | YOUTH WRITER

My sister first taught me how to smile in photos.

For years, toothache counted out the whites, brushed my face with untraceable discontent. Ticked the corners of my mouth; aching cheeks; let's see those pearly whites.

Then she stood by my side and . Ssqueezed the excess skin on my elbow. That's when our bodies turned T.V. static, earthquake shoulders we pressed against one another as we tried to remain upright. Our laughter transported us through the frame; now our walls are elbow-deep in scrunched noses and upturned mouths.

She taught me how to heal, too.

Helped me close my eyes, and brave let the pill tip-toeing down my throat trickle with water. The burning sensation of a clogged throat washed away with the steady pulse of her hand. Half my size. Twice as strong. And when the trickle transferred to my cheeks, her lap became a tear-stained canvas. My sister made something beautiful out of the heavy, damp, and darkdarkness.

11 years old. Just like Miah Cerillo, life-cord tethered to her friends' death, red-glazestained memories painting over existing artwork normal. A ghost of 'daddy's little girl', face cold; hard. Metal- like the shots that fire at the end of every period. Every exclamation- turned- statement -turned- question, because nothing is certain anymore.

How do they feel around for beauty in the dark when their limbs are weighed with metal bullets?

When they woke up that morning, to gunshots echoing sounded like clanging-crashing pots and pans. Like mommy's eggs smeared on the floor, like a glass vase too fractured for flowers.

When they left home that morning, "I love you" rested on was a comma, followed by "see you later".

When they got to school that morning, white walls were plastered with all-about-me's and thank-you notes. With letters to pen pals and secret drawings pulled from desk drawers and framed. When the clock struck 11:33 AM, desks became shields, lifelines, too thin to drown out a muffled cry. Walls were suddenly exposed, now tinted, tainted, no longer pure.

"I love you" wasn't meant to be a eulogy.

Uziyah Garcia
Makenna Elrod
Jose Flores
Xavier Lopez
Amerie Garza
Tessy Mata
Alexandria Rubio
Nevaeh Bravo
Miranda Mathis

—Their names spill over a news headline. Too many to say in one breath, one last breath they never had.

Your son could be next. Your cousin, your student, our sisters. Our lives could be rooted with cavities, cheek-aching toothache smiles returned. The steady pulse of a hand half our size overtaken by a soundless echo. How do we heal when there's no one left to teach us how?

TAXONOMY OF IDENTITY

ADESIYAN OLUWAPELUMI | NIGERIA

Kingdom:
I am a cadet of earned identities;
never myself, for myself, by myself,
but a pseudonym for the paradox
of belonging I lodge in the confines
of my leathered flesh.
We all wear a coat of privilege & I,
careless seamstress, weave broken
pastiche into the fabric of my being.
Behind every weft is a loose fray.

Phylum:
The flag whipped its wings like a ready
predator; its sharp fangs teething at
us with a solemn sneer.
Countries paying royalties to the slavery of
independence. We term what will
cage and not kill us — freedom.
That's the only way we can adulterate this
war song; that it may taste like an
anthem of conquered peace.
The truth is this:
the battle still lingers in our
throats like a bullet, anxious in its cartridge.

Class:
Around a burnt steak, hunters herd,
hands clasped in the hinges of another.
We learn to hold the ghost of ourselves
and hear them speak the silent dialect.
Silence, so heavy its gravity falls on
the weight of our deaf eyes. We listen
with raptness, the melody of a song
that dyes its solfa with the satin paint
of Beethovenian sonatas.

Order:
Tribes congregate in front of the firing
squad; our borders confluence in the
terrain of death. I walk the same steps
as a Hausa girl & we
share a common death.

Family:
Hierarchy is in the numbers
and here we do not count ghosts.
Bodies illuminated by absence.
I was told you arrived in Seraph's
wings, Son of Zion. Do you pity me?
Is your sympathy a testament
of the body I carry. I mean, do you
die for generic humans like me, unsure

of their mortality. Lord, I am not
cherubic, I think myself an offspring
of a god. I think myself a god.

Genus:
The world is a room stacked with
imprisoning rights. We girdle the fetters
of our language around our tongues
and our utterances suddenly become
screams. At the Fifth National Congress,
a woman stood with dagger eyes and poniyard posture above
masculine seats, & they plunge her
blade into her cavities.
Say our bodies undo us when it pleases.

Species:
I am the last of my generation
at the end of everything — seeking....

THE LOCKDOWN WALK

SURESWARI BAGH, TRANSLATED BY PITAMBAR NAIK | INDIA

My feet are sturdy.
I had forgotten
I'd never walked that far
and that long, in a single stretch.

I was making bricks
kneading the clay with feet
I was moving the earth.

Taking the feet forward,
I was ploughing and
with the endurance of the fire
I'd learnt to be ash.

Letting my feet not tire
I've built many palaces for you

oh, master
I was walking only for you
over the years, but this time,
you made me walk for myself.

NO EQUAL(ITY)

SUSAN L. LIN | USA

They razed sugarcane fields
to erect the bones that formed
our neighborhood schools, but never
taught us the truth buried in the land:
that the bedrock of our education was built
over unmarked graves of slave laborers;
that the skeletons of those incarcerated souls
might never be uncovered as the town flourished
and the foundation spread.

Living bodies spilled out of buildings
too small to contain their growing numbers,
so the grounds became a perpetual construction zone.
Annex after annex: classrooms where we learned
about nearby prisons and factories led to cafeterias
where we sprinkled crystals from sugar packets
onto our palms, unaware of the invisible chains
that stretched across the passage in between,
unaware of the trapped past at rest beneath the soles
of our small feet.

MERCILESS MERCENARY

GOODWELL KAIPA | MALAWI

It troubles me to see mounds

Now as dry as a granite stone

A reminder that you came not to play

But to deprive us of those we hold dear

Don't your fangs go blunt from your insatiable hunger?

You who wreaks havoc unspeakable

A merciless mercenary on crusade to annihilate

Leaving behind wailing orphans

Their parents prematurely nipped from the bud

Owing to your virulent nature

Campaigns against you crop up now and again

Yet your victims accumulate like speed bumps

Mounds in the ground

You a victorious warrior

You an epidemic that has spared no household

PLASTIC

HEC LAMPERT-BATES | USA

There's a man eating plastic on 6th and Green. I walked past him four times this week, often on route to my job at Tri-Trifle, but I'll admit the later passes were fueled by curiosity. There's a man sitting on the curb, eating plastic straws outside the restaurant at the corner of 6th and Green.

I noticed him on Monday. I hadn't lived a day as warm. My neck was spitting mist and my new white socks were baked in dry sweat. I paused beside the man as a cloud of workers straggled past. He sat hunched, yellow-gloved fingers around a container of straws, and a bag for empty wrappers. His loafers sank through melted divots in the concrete. I leaned in to inspect what was either a mustache, or a bush of twigs taped to his upper lip — I'm still not sure which. I cleared my throat. He was busy and ignored me. He stuffed the last three straws between his teeth, stood and retrieved another box from behind a tree. I coughed again, but he was busy.

On Tuesday, I told my wife about him, but you know Daurene. She's always been a skeptic. She didn't believe my stories about the leeches last summer, or the one about my friend who made cooking oil from lead paint, so naturally, she had no interest in the plastic man. I even suggested she come with me and make a day of it. We could watch him for a while and maybe go to a movie after. But Daurene didn't have time. She was absorbed in whatever start-up she had concocted that week — selling reusable socks or something.

So I called Fred, my old pal. I didn't know Fred was in the hospital. Why did no one tell me Fred was in the hospital? Some cyst on his foot? Apparently he's been there for months. He hung up when I asked if I could wheel him to see the man. Why didn't anyone tell me Fred was hospitalized?

On Wednesday, alone and disappointed, I walked past the man again and feigned interest in that over-soaked ice cream next door with its olives and curdle, so he wouldn't think I was odd.

I never would have expected a straw to crunch. I suppose it makes sense for plastic between teeth to sound like leaves and apples and celery, but I was astounded by my mouth as it dribbled lust for the man's plastic. The way it crunched, its slight chew, the supple rip of molded oil. I thought, before I remembered sense, I might taste one. Just to help him. But I didn't. I walked on like I hadn't seen him and salty rain sank through my hair.

Thursday was wet.

When I rose from the subway and found my way to him, I'd almost finished convincing myself I was there on business.

"Excuse me," I said, and waved my foot near his nose. He peeled the sides of a particularly long straw, a manufactured banana without all the things you would want from fruit. I nudged a woman with purple boots and eyebrows separated by a large pimple, as she hobbled by. She spun, shocked like a mouse with a freshly pulled tail.

"Do you know who this is?" I asked the woman.

She puzzled and scrunched her eyebrows together, leaking white muck down her nose. She whispered "Don't stare at the homeless," and scuttled away, dripping a rich path behind her.

When I arrived on Friday, I was delighted to find others. Four workers stood in a bubble around the man, using fingers and torn documents to shield their eyes from the storm. I dropped my case with its brevity and importance and ran to the crowd.

"What's happening?" I asked and shoved through. No one knew. We just stood and watched a man in a vest and high stockings eat plastic straws. Every few minutes, the crack of a dropped satchel and a new watcher would split the group. By the time he'd eaten four boxes, the corner of 6th and Green was surrounded like ants spiral a stale crumb. I wish Daurene and Fred could have seen.

We huddled until I couldn't stand any longer. Across the circle was the woman from Thursday. Her face was clean and her eyes were stuck to the back of his neck. I couldn't stay or leave. Confusion had turned my brain fuzzy and soft. What if he did something? Or nothing? Or, what if I died that night and would never know?

Horrible rain.

I took a breath and approached the man with velvet steps, eager not to spook him. "Why?" I asked. Everyone stopped breathing and blinking and moving and all the things that could prevent an answer.

He put down his box and stared at me through the flimsy eyes of a tired man. He shrugged. "Fifteen dollars an hour."

The clouds broke.

THRESHOLD

HEATHER SALUTI | CANADA

landlords, with their insatiable thirst for pestilence
knock at our door.
we hold them shut to protect our bodies
like duvets filled with down-discretion,
plucked to shield intrusive eyes from our rarity
treasures of framed occasions
that reveal how to be
human.

landlords, barely masking their horntails
hide behind re-used plasticity
far away from the written word their evasion belittles
our lived experience.
they offer us small distractions
— synthetic upgrade promises
already broken, pest
traps too small to slaughter
salivating developers,
a green organics bin to store
banana peels & our renoviction fear
when will they wave
over their hats, turn
our housing to mulch?

CACTI LEFT TO BLOOM

PURABI BHATTACHARYA | INDIA

"I was scared all the time. They said drop the case. I did not relent,"
read a headline of a newspaper.
You read the story to the final line. Full stop.
You run, race away, deify silence, playing the gardener.
With flooded eyes you dig deep into the earth;
let it soak in the dirty blood,
streaming out of the cunt.

With halting, jarring language,
stories of incredible pain, preserved with black ink and salt;
you let your tears scribble upon the daily headline.
White no longer chastens.

Every blot bonds. Salt. Sweat. Sanguine fluid;
Your innards now a man-modelled map;
the cartographer of this land plants a cactus to bloom.
You become the stockpile safekeeping his spit and his debris;
Once a pluviophile, you have become deadpan to petrichor
Soon the nights blur. In a dark sky, a well star lit takes pity;
its stillness turns you deaf. You are invisible.

With each dawn, when you open your eyes, you know
a brook, a stream, a river, a sea has no closure for you.

LOSING IT

CYNDY MUSCATEL | USA

As you get older, you get afraid you're losing it. Take for example that you don't remember where you put your car keys or, for that matter, your car. If you're younger, you're just annoyed. If you're older, you think you're losing it. You call it a senior moment, forgetting all the times in the past when you'd be late to work because you couldn't find your keys. Or when you wandered around the Costco parking lot looking for your car in the blazing sun.

I talked about this to my neighbor the other day. I'd come out of the house to take our dog for a walk. Nina was standing in front of her garage with her daughter, who is in medical school. Neither had a clue where the keys to their car were. Nina had her sunglasses on—her reading glasses were on top of her head. I didn't know if I should point that out. I had a feeling if I didn't, she'd be starting a new game of hide and seek.

"I'm always losing things," she confessed as she put her glasses into her purse. "Like when I can't find my phone and I realize I'm talking into it." She laughed.

That's what you do when you're younger. You laugh. When I was looking for my phone the other day and found it in my hand, I got scared. If you're older, you keep it to yourself because you're afraid—afraid your kids will find out and insist on power of attorney.

I admit I'm a bit scatterbrained. My brain is like a fast-moving freeway lane crowded with bumper-to-bumper thoughts running through it. I have quite a history of leaving things cooking on the stove—hard-boiled eggs are my specialty. I've done it on and off for years, much to the detriment of my pots and my kitchen. Once it was chicken breasts. I was going to make us chicken salad before we went to see the movie Seabiscuit, so I had four chicken breasts simmering in a small pot. When my husband hurried me out the door, I forgot about them. It was only during the movie, when the family on screen was eating chicken, that I remembered.

"We've got to go home now," I whispered to my husband.

"But the movie's not over," he said

I stood up. "I read the book so I know the ending. And I left chicken on the stove."

We made it home minutes before disaster struck. Nothing caught on fire but the house was filled with smoke, which took days to clear. The four chicken breasts looked like toasted marshmallows that had stayed too long in the campfire. And the pan? Forgetta 'bout it.

If that happened at my age now, I'm afraid it won't be the fire department pounding on my door but welfare services coming to cart me off to assisted living. And I'd be put in a room that didn't have a kitchenette. That's why I instituted a new rule: If I'm boiling eggs I must stay in the kitchen until they are done. It works out well unless I get distracted reading headlines on my iPad.

I lost my wedding ring once. I have a habit of sliding my ring off and on, which I was doing in the back seat of a friend's car. The ring slipped and fell off my finger. We searched that car top to bottom but never found it. Until the day my friend had her dryer vent cleaned out. That happened thirty years ago. No one could figure out how it got there. If it happened now, I'd be sure my mind was playing tricks on me. I'd know I was losing it.

SOMEHOW WHEN I GO ON THE INTERNET, THERE ARE LOTS OF ARTICLES ABOUT ALZHEIMER'S POSTED ON MY PAGE. TO COUNTERACT THE IMPLICIT THREAT TO MY BRAIN, I STARTED DOING BRAIN GAMES.

I'm not very lucky at games. I take that back. I'm unlucky at games. I started playing bridge but I had to quit. I never got enough points in a hand to make a bid. Being dummy only has so much allure. When my grandson, Evan, was three, he crushed me at the card game War. He patted me on my hand, saying, "Grammy, we can get you lessons!" My luck hasn't changed with the passage of years. Recently my six-year-old granddaughter beat me forty-one games in a row playing Candyland.

But give me a game like Scrabble that's all about words, I'm hard to beat. Enter Words With Friends! During the COVID-19 shutdown, I became addicted. Many afternoons were spent dueling with friends. My competitive streak was as out of control as my screen time.

Lumosity is another Internet game I play. A Facebook friend suggested it to help keep the mental cylinders firing, but it has taught me much more: I've learned the art of focus. I can now keep my mind on the task at hand rather than thinking in several other directions. Which is a plus for a random-abstract thinker.

Until I was getting into my car at Costco yesterday, I had a cutesy conclusion written for this essay. It started with "Getting older is not for sissies." But as I put my items in the trunk, I realized I hadn't had any trouble knowing where I'd parked. I'd done several errands before and hadn't needed a list. I still walk three miles a day and now play pickleball. I head a committed on a Foundation board. So what do I have to be afraid of? Nothing, except the prejudice of ageism. I've fallen in the trap of stereotyping myself as "the Medicare person," someone who isn't healthy physically or cognitively.

I'm going to lose it.

INVERTED TRIANGLE BODY

ARINA ALAM

WEST BENGAL

INDIA

A simple remark can raise the whirl of those anxious worms.
A simple gesture of laughter can feed those worms,
my groundhog days like green leaves.
I am an inverted triangle Body
Not a hourglass, not even a pear
I don't even fit in the square.

A simple body, an abode of the soul
That's scrutinized by conventional lenses.
Oblong head, broad shoulders
Tiny legs are declared not so feminine.
Asymmetrical eyes , thin lips,
Protruding chins are not so feline.
A Whimsical art created by The God.
A revolt against the conventional Beauty Rules.

The thread of conventional beauty standards
sits upon my neck and suffocates my breath.
I explain daily to my therapist:
How many weird stares have passed,
how many jokes have been cracked,
how many questions have been raised about my gender identity.

I pop pills to accept my body.
I let them dissect my body
like a frog on morphine.
Half unconscious in dreams for a desirable mold.
A dying wish to fit in,
A whispered prayer for a miracle to happen.

MEDITATIONS IN A FRACTURED ARCHIPELAGO

ALYZA TAGUILASO | PHILIPPINES

Today I receive boxes of things I have no time

to pick up myself. Red car jack, garbage

bags, a bucket of candy, a book of a friend

living halfway across the Pacific. At work, we get patients

who are shot, one tried to hang herself with a red ribbon

used to wrap a box of cake. Some get better, others don't make it

past a few hours. Once, someone was brought in

pulseless after being suffocated

under heaps of flour. We are sorry

for your loss is usually cut short

by someone's sobbing. Spouse, mother, sister, son,

friend. A few years ago, I thought the world ended

and I wouldn't have to think of people and their patterns and

how exhausted this world makes me. Muscle, bone, sinew, vessel,

nerve. Scrub, scalpel, incise, rinse, repeat. Don't forget

to take your home medications. Here I stand, awake

at 6 am, stretching my limbs as the earth remains

dry and parched under our feet. Bones sandwiched

between soil, rock, and oil. What treasures do these unnamed graves hold?

What calamities and plagues had they witnessed before their souls fossilized
with regret? In my country, when it rains, cities flood. We thrive
on monuments of mud and weeping. Mountain ranges
scalped bare by industry. Diwatas driven away
by drought. Profit for whose greater good? Greed grows
its exit wounds on almost all corners of this nation. Once I read
how a healed femur was the first sign of civilization; community.
But even that turned out to be fake news, manufactured
and spread by people desperate to get high on hope at the height
of the pandemic. Here is a broken bone. If you stop moving,
it might heal. Otherwise, it remains
fractured like the earth. Speaking
in tremors and quakes. Refusing
to answer to all names
we utter to appease it.

FIVE HORSES

TYLER HEIN | CANADA

Pestilence was directing traffic by flinging arrows at the heels of slow walkers along my morning commute. Bless her. The world is less of a drag since everyone started walking about fifteen percent quicker for fear of loitering too long in raw air. I follow her on social, mainly because of her horse. She's always posing with him, his decaying body, its partially visible skeleton, the grim smile of exposed skull.

Pestilence was the first of the four to appear, a few years back now. Honestly, I can't really remember the time before. So much has happened since her arrival that it's reduced my memory to swirling fragments of light and shadow like a faulty camera. Pestilence is a bit of a nuisance, but she's endurable. Hell, many of us welcomed her. She thinned out traffic, and the empty roads gave us all a place to put our loneliness. Now, War. War is a different story.

It's ridiculous what we allow him to get away with, especially once he usurped leadership of the police. Now he personally investigates and clears any wrongdoing by him and his department. I guess violence built into the system never counts as violence so he's free to tramp around the neighbourhood with a fiery sword hacking down anyone who gets too near or pushes too hard against the margins. The last few months has seen him embark on a tour of the talk-show circuit. Sometimes I fall asleep listening to War moan about his problems with addictions, latent trauma, trouble at home, the stress of the job, how if we'd all just follow the rules it wouldn't need to be this way. It's plainly obvious he's trying to rebrand his image because he hasn't been able to get laid (which has only made him more brutal by the way). He has his diehards, but I can't stand the guy. He's the reason I'm even going into work today.

My manager called me ranting about how we were understaffed. Apparently War bisected Devon for calling him 'maidenless' at a protest outside the police department. I'll miss the guy, he was good craic, but he should have known better than to poke at power. Even if Devon wasn't publicly shredded there would have been another reason. It's always something with somebody. Nobody wants to work. And why would they? I don't, that's for sure. But ever since Famine moved into my building the price of rent and groceries shot into the stratosphere like a Bezos rocket, so the superiors know I'll come whenever they call because I can barely pay the weekly interest premiums on my student loans. Most everyone I know is stuck in this limbo, of working double to go half. It's a bitter pill to swallow, having a whole generation realize en masse that we're dogs stuck chasing a ball that was never thrown.

I'M TOLD I'M LUCKY SINCE I EVEN HAVE A JOB.

I've worked at the same restaurant for nearly ten years. The walls are covered in pictures of old Presidents and most of the staff are nice in a paid sort-of-way. About a year ago it was bought by Disney, repackaged as part of their Disney+ lifestyle subscription, and now taking selfies inside it is considered culturally necessary, so now it's filled with a mix of the new gentry (celebrities, YouTube critics, social media mavens) and the dregs (nurses, teachers, ugly children).

My manager was waiting at front of house. I apologized profusely for not realizing I might be needed. He made sure to wipe his soles on the carpet before raising each foot closer to my lips when I bent to kiss his shoes. He's one of the good ones. On Sundays he pretends not to see me sneaking bites from the guest's unfinished plates before I toss the leftovers into the incinerator. Nobody eats for free on in the House of Mouse.

Death was already seated in my section, munching on his second bowl of complimentary bread. I used to be star-struck by him because, like, whoa, he's Death, but now not so much. He's always here, I swear. Seeing Death doesn't strike the same awe it once did, and he's aware that something about being up close to him elicits a gentle pity. He looked so paltry alone in the booth, breadcrumbs rock sliding down his chest. Just another lonely old man yearning for carriage back to his more virile past, to when people would fawn and beg and sing the praises of big bad Death and his super scary infinite nothing. I wasn't in a stroking sort of mood. What's supposed to be such a raw deal about him anyway? What end is he even the harbinger of? The four of them came down, and I stayed clocking into work. It puts the end into perspective a bit, don't you think?

A FAMILIAR SOUND

SABAHAT ALI WANI | KASHMIR

It was a terrible year. The place was rotting away and the people populating the miserable land were ill and diseased. Shafiyah sat down on a chair and began cleaning the outer sole of her shoes with a small fallen tree branch.

A decaying, rain-soaked land amidst mountains was not the ideal place to complete her research thesis at all but she had chosen this for herself. She understood the weight of this research, even if no one else did. She was in a fever, a place full of undivided focus, where doubt, comfort, and luxury didn't dare to enter.

While cleaning her shoes, she scrunched her nose, considering the flesh that must have dissolved itself in the mud, clinging to her.

She threw the branch away and stood up to walk towards her apartment.

The surroundings that welcomed her were typical, dull, and repetitive. A group of men sitting together and discussing how women and their unveiled heads were responsible for the plague; a tea maker putting more water in milk so that he could earn more out of it; two dogs sitting on the pavement waiting for the animal lovers to give them some food; wrappers of injections piled up on one side of the road while the other side was reserved for household waste; worried mothers carrying their children to the nearest facility for a checkup.

There was a hazy, conglomeration of smells. Of smoke and medicines.

Shafiyah hated both. She covered her nose with a piece of cloth and rushed to her place.

Once she stepped inside and closed the door behind her, she took the Hijab off her head that she had worn to save herself from acid attacks and death threats. She was not a believer and never wanted to cover her head with some cloth to prove her modesty, innocence, and virginity. When she turned nine, her mother forced her to wear it and then, she was threatened by her brothers to cover her head, claiming that if she didn't, they would shave it off. Now, no woman could go out without wearing a Hijab because a bullet, a rapist, a bottle of acid, or sexually repressed religious lunatics were just a few moments away from performing their holy duties and getting a reserved spot in the land of paradise.

She clutched the floral printed Hijab in her hand and moved towards the dressing corner.

Decompressing in the chair in front of the mirror, she let out a heavy breath.

Releasing the cloth from her hand, it fell to the ground. She pressed her fingers to her forehead to ease some of her worries. She was worried but not afraid. Since she had left her parent's house, she was not scared of anything. Always cautious, but never scared.

She didn't miss her family. She waited for the feeling of longing to arrive but it never did. It felt liberating. It gave her the relief one gets after the amputation of a nasty aching organ.

SHE SHIFTED ON THE CHAIR AND LOOKED AT HER FACE IN THE MIRROR.

Even if she didn't miss her family, her face, sprinkled with freckles and topped with an unignorable crooked nose always reminded her of the people who held the same features as her.

Suddenly, with no courtesy of warning, she felt the walls closing on her. She knew what was happening.

Sweat broke out on her skin and she could feel the irritation brewing in her chest.

She knew that this irritation would turn into suffocation in a matter of seconds and then, she would have to patiently wait for it to end.

She didn't have any medicine for it. She was used to just dealing with it on her own.

It was not over. She could still feel her heart thumping violently inside her chest.

'Just a few more seconds', she kept on repeating to herself.

She pushed herself off of her chair and started moving toward her bed. Her knees not strong enough either to take her to the comfort of her bed.

She compromised with her body and fell on the floor of her room.

She moved her limbs to find a position less of an instigation to her headache.

She could hear the people who lived downstairs—the clatter of utensils indicating that it was already dinner time, giggles of two daughters whom the parents didn't want when they were born, and a continuous sound, a ticking one. Something was going off in their house.

Their dinner preparations reminded Shafiyah that she had to cook something too. After this unavoidable fit, she decided to prepare a good meal for herself. That's the first sign of being a responsible adult. Never skip meals; it would do you no good.

Her heart calmed ever slightly and she took this chance to sit up.

With her hands between her legs and her head dangling at an awkward angle, she could feel the saliva coming out of her mouth. Long slimy ropes covered her mouth, chin, and neck.

What an erotic sight, she humoured herself. It was a sensual dance of saliva on the beats of her throbbing head and thumping heart, accompanied by her buzzing skin and longing for medicine instead of a lover.

She wiped off the saliva with the sleeve of her shirt and stood up.

She rolled the saliva-covered sleeves of her shirt and moved toward the kitchen.

She took her time to reach the sink and opened the tap with no franticity.

As her hands made contact with the water, relief hit her body. She cleaned her face and opened her rolled sleeves to wash them too of all the saliva and sweat.

After she made herself clean enough to cook, Shafiyah thought of preparing a good fulfilling meal.

She decided to make it exactly how her mother used to prepare it for her except for the cinnamon. She didn't like cinnamon in her food. It made drinks better but in food, meat especially; it overpowered every other spice and herb. Anything but cinnamon.

While she was cutting the vegetables for the broth, she couldn't hear the ticking sound and the people downstairs were also silent.

As she put the vegetables in oil, Shafiyah moved back a little on instinct. She added all the necessary spices to the mix and let it cook after adding some water. The aroma of spices had slowly started filling up her apartment and she felt a lot better.

'Should I cook an egg too?' she thought.

She looked in her fridge and found none. With a sigh, she closed the door of the fridge. As her hand released the door handle, a seering pain shot up her arm and she quickly pulled her hand back.

She saw that her skin was burnt.

'When did this happen? What burnt my skin?' she shockingly wondered.

In the same breath, she started coughing.

She raised her head to take in her surroundings and realised that her room was filled with smoke. Irritation started bubbling inside the walls of her throat again and she began scratching her neck vigorously.

The ticking sound was back.

In a room filled with smoke, Shafiyah lept towards the stovetop and turned off the gas.

She rushed towards the door and opened it, gasping for air.

The reality waited, stark, for her through the open door. .

Nothing. No smoke, no sirens, no crowd, nothing hinting at the fire blazing in the building.

Taking two fast steps to catch the railing, Shafiyah tilted herself at an angle to look into the family's house downstairs.

Her panic-filled face was in complete contrast with the calm and silent scene of their house.

It was a moment of realization for Shafiyah. She couldn't bring up the courage to look at her room because she knew what she will find.

Nothing, again.

Her condition had evolved. She was used to hallucinations and bizarre illusions but at that moment, the degree of realness in the whole period made her more anxious.

Her hands were not burnt, there was no smoke and the night had fallen on the valley. However, the ticking sound was present. Shafiyah clutched the railing tightly when it fell upon her that the ticking sound was an extension of this cruelty.

It was an alarm in the still-alive corners of her mind, wanting her to escape the phase of ridiculous illusions and take refuge in the arms of some medicine. It was her body's desperate attempt at bringing her back.

The stark contradiction between her and the surroundings was vivid, almost brutal to accept.

She brought her body down and placed her head on the railing.

Her breathing had reached the normal state and she could trust her body to balance on its own.

As the rainy winds sprinkled a few drops of water on her face, she felt a little grateful toward the perishing land. It might be dying a slow death but it still showered love and mercy on the inhabitants on certain occasions like this one.

She looked around her and felt relief at the normalcy of everything.

The smell of rotten meat was normal. The smell of mud was safe. The persistence of cowardly silence was home.

EUCHARIST I

NWUGURU CHIDIEBERE SULLIVAN | NIGERIA

(i)
Loss is a burnt thumb that tricks our skin into cenotaphs.
The only road that opens into us is a hand that shreds
flowers for scents; people here do this a lot to perceive
themselves saints. What are we waiting for before we
give it all up; I mean, to the up above?— an offering
to the ineptitude of a god sleeping on us.

(ii)
Ever believed that soldiers could troop
into armless hamlets & spread storms
poisoned with bullets as an offer from
the government? Headless corpses forfeit
the biddings from the wind, pollute the
soil with their grievance, uplift their
burdened souls from the ground where
their pink fingers make shapeless
signatures with bloody inks.

(iii)

Heads howling, homes burning. I took a bow from the newspaper stand where the headlines line the heads of the newly bereaved. The president must be warming up to offer a handful of odds on a life-support to the masses. Call here a nirvana & watch us rise to claim it. We dare not riot or we'll be declared "shoot on sight."

(iv)

Hopes crumble until there's none left, the faith that should be standing on our arms have fallen close to our feet & these limbless dreams, these dreams should be standing on prosthetic limbs but to whose end do we make it? Loss should be earned, I screamed to the flaccid ghouls milking our lives for the taste of it:

May today not be our end!

EUCHARIST II

NWUGURU CHIDIEBERE SULLIVAN | NIGERIA

Loss still glitters like a neon bulb.
Tomorrow comes too quick at us
& we are never prepared for it.
Possibilities give no fuck about us.

IT IS TOMORROW ALREADY

Buttoned in between the belly of
handicaps of life & the stillness
of death; the brackets curling up for
the first time into multiple-choice questions
& we're still the only ones left out.

Imagine this: a cyborg hacking into
a fruitless heart. The nation skyrocketing
into a misplaced history, rigged elections
& upturned victories in favour of those
bribing karma.

This is no movie; the villain still wins,
the vampires still perform the eucharist
of blood, & I'm no zombie to go after
the brains behind this. I let them win,
after all, loss glitters like a neon bulb.

HAIL & BRIMSTONES IN SUDAN

ADESINA AJALA | NIGERIA

The Poem in Which the Silent Agonies of Trapped Souls Gnash Teeth

Dark clouds gather & hail & brimstones fall in Sudan. Come,
come & see everyone running into things tender & haunting:
A baby is running into the hushed sighs of her mother. Her mother says
in Arabic, Fi alharb, la takul abdan ma yakfi. She says, In war, you don't eat enough.
A father is running into worthless currencies & unmet needs. The taps are
running out of water & thirst is widening, like an ocean gyre,
into torments. The embassies are running into the bellies
of cargo planes. Ghost streets sprout from noisy places. This poem is
running too, it is running me into enjambed imageries smeared with burnt flesh.
On Eid day, the muezzin's voice runs weary on empty fields in Darfur. Ramadan
ends in gun sounds & bullets ricocheting off hospital walls. In Khartoum,
a RSF soldier points gun at a fellow Sudanese in army wears & sputters blood
graffiti on a wall. A chick is snuggling round the carcass of its mother. Poet,
pray the soul of Sudan does not fall prey to itself. I watch a
Nigerian student begs to make it home in a TikTok video, & I enter
into a poem half done, because a war threatening my countryman
is not a fair muse. But let this poem save me first. This poem in which the silent
agonies of trapped souls gnash teeth like a child trembling with fever.

UNTOUCHABILITY

MACKENZIE DUAN | USA | YOUTH WRITER

"It would be all right if we only raped them. I shouldn't say all right. But we always stabbed and killed them. Because dead bodies don't talk." — *Shiro Azuma*

for Iris Chang

Under a roof
of war photos. I can't.

Let go: the tulip
graves. Soldier

peeling off underwear.
No one

knows: a villager
buried to the hilt of their head.

Then dogs. Clock
of shrapnel. Did you know?

Did you
want? To know:
a Nazi saved

Nanjing. Eyewitness

to the breakage
of babies in the river.

Correction: tanks
shearing a forest.

The soldiers
competed

for kills. Crowned
dogs. I want ending.

Still nothing
ends, the arc
of the bayonet
mid-painting. Japan

apologizes
fifty years after. Denial

willowed
into mask, another shrill

tax of unending.
Correction: there were no walls,

only the fact of human

bodies. Trained to see us

as animals. Wrong
simile. I can't.

Unthink: the woman's
mouth in a ruched O,

schools oranged
by hand grenade. This plait

of testimony. Soldiers
die unguilty:

of winning. Survival
creeping to an end

as beasts whimper
below dirt. Correction:

below a wind of killers.
Nothing wrong

with immortality. Only I can't
unstomach. The true

meat of their selves. I can't
fire. An arrow

notched with their names.

Gunshot wound

like a pupil, widening, mirroring
apology, marrying

night. Correction:
all soldiers

are taught. Correction:
to apologize

is to desire ending. Correction:
so many words

lost in a red channel
of civilians. In the lie

of gun shells. Their organs
inverted by dogs. Violet '

retinas. An etymology
of corpses. Correction:

I inherited their anatomy,
those carbon litanies. Every apology

already unwinding. Their fists
still open

in the end.

PURPLE BLOUSE

UZOMAH UGWU
USA

BY NIGHT SHE RAN

A purple blouse caught in between wires
A girl once wore while escaping a part of life
That froze in the heat

Bushes held images that still flee
Body parts mirrored in different sexes
She left because she couldn't mention

Who she was in broken houses
A man is not a woman and a woman is not a man
Her people left her out at dawn
So by night, she ran

Not knowing how to exit but
only knowing why

She began leaving parts of her that
her culture and country denied
she found a way so she could be herself
and not question why

she held the road tight like a right of passage
she ran fast from what she knew so she could be
what she needed to become and grow like a rose

outside the fence to freedom
what got caught who knows but she needed to move on
and left the purple blouse and forget who she was

MOTHER NEVER DIES

BASUDEV SUNANI, TRANSLATED BY PITAMBAR NAIK | INDIA

Has anyone ever heard of or seen a mother dying?
Man dies but Mother never.

She is always present, in the eyes when alive
and at the end, in the chest.
She comforts every orphan in her saree drape.

Which is why we call our land, our nation, Mother.

When a mother dies, the soil cracks and
what remains but a nation absent of
Mother's affection and fondness.

After eons, perhaps a mother's gravestone is not
hiding in any shanty or any unknown village's field

rather beside the national railway track
in the sunlight, in front of crores of people.
It's astonishing that whether or not the soil
has cracked, whether or not the nation has broken

her touch has reached the crores of
orphans and ignorant children of the nation.

I MET AMERICA

UZOMAH UGWU | USA

I met America but she rejected me
Her laws, her rules. She threw the book at me

Outlaws of humanity America made me
Scars she carved in my soul that

This would never be my home
I met America and set foot on her soil

But she didn't want me to stay the
way I came. America was not brave or free for me

I met America and she said I didn't
Look American to her. So I should leave.

E. PALESTINE OHIO

ARYA F. JENKINS | USA

There's a thick black plume of toxic smoke
Wending its way somewhere
Black smoke that obfuscates
Confuses like all mistakes
And horrors we would rather set aside
Than understand

They try to unravel what went down
With reassuring words
But can't undo what's done
Or cover it up because
They care more about the price of poison
Than what it does

This is what happened
This is what we should not have done
This is what we will no longer do
This is what we can do now

Instead black smoke
Lies and poison no one can stop
Seeping into our water
Infiltrating our homes
Worrying our skin and bones

> **IT FEELS LIKE THERE'S NOWHERE TO GO LIKE EVEN THE AIR OUTSIDE HAS TURNED AGAINST US.**

PLEASE LEAVE ON

DAWN MACDONALD
CANADA

IN 1989

AT

3 P.M.

The teachers all wrote p.L.O.
In the chalkboard's corners
And we said, "that means
Palestine liberation organization,"
Because we knew so much.

Our wisdom was the kind
that's learned in Current Events.
Current Events was the first five
minutes of Social Studies
class and the Social Studies
teacher was known to be dating a student.
We all said, "That's gross."

We got in trouble for looking
out the window and for reading
unassigned texts. We said,
"You'll get the strap," and,
"Nuh, they outlawed corporal
punishment," and, "I heard one kid
still got it."

We got seated separately
from our friends and found ways
to exchange notes. The sky
was so full of ice, it fell apart.
We lost heat from our heads.
We knew several facts, and whether
to repeat them. They had us set
for life.

WHEN YOU ASK ME FOR LEVITY

TANIA CHEN | MEXICO

It starts like this: I always dream of little open mouths at the bottom grounds for my execution. They're simple: oval-shaped openings with overcrowded rows of pearly whites. If you look closely I might see the chewed-up leftover of a crooked phalanx or a meaty hamstring or even intestines coiling along.

The grounds for my execution are 3,145 kilometers (1,954 miles) of silver barbed wire; mausoleum cement raised barricades; and then, the endless sand dunes like undulating waves. All the way down the beach and into the sea, cleaving the land in two.

With their lack of human footprints, they deceive you into running ahead. Trick you into forgetting that the grounds for my execution are lined with rows of nailed coffins on aluminum walls: year, number, muertes.

The rattlesnakes like coiled traps waiting to spring up; the saguaro providing a sliver of shade, thin like the butcher knife of our abuela. And behind me is just el Rio Grande, as we kick our feet along the waters of the ground for my execution, a storm of painted ladies making the journey overhead. They sail north, then south, and will be the only witnesses at the end.

I pray they'll take my soul with them. Virgencita, Virgen de Guadalupe or, if she fails me, Santa Muerte ven por mí, no me dejes morir sola aquí.

The grounds for your execution, you say, with levity in your voice, and napkin smeared with mole: Do Not Cross, there is nothing there worth dying for.

                              Like you've forgotten what we're running from.

A MOTHER'S OATH

TASNEEM HOSSAIN | BANGLADESH

In the dark, cold summer storm,
She sits wishing for a free life.
Hopeful eyes watching the lightning;
Her child sleeps on the hay stack bed,
The strong wind caressing her hair.

In the mud house her restless soul yearns for love.
Love that could fulfill her hopes and dreams,
Take care of all her miseries.
Let her heart to be carefree.
The freezing night's hands strangle her throat-
Breathless she screams.
No voice heard.
The falling water droplets now,
Cry in mournful howls.
The winds thumping on the window,
Sing the dark night's song.
Her face stiffens, she knows;

She picks the tiny little bag,
Tells her daughter to awake;
The storm inside her is strong,
Stronger than the night storm;

She takes a last look at the dusty room.
Today will be the last day of her unseen shackled days.
They cannot remain a slave;
Outside, she steps to a journey unknown.

The fiery soul knows, the road ahead is pebbly.
She has to change her daughter's destiny.
She must make her daughters life worthy and free.
She smiles; the smile of a determined soul.
The mother in her knows it all.

Tomorrow will be fine...

KINDERGARTEN IN RUSSIA

ROBERT PETTUS | UNITED STATES & RUSSIA

The creaking elevator dinged shut. I pressed the first-floor button. The lift slid wobbling unstably downward from my small apartment on the thirteenth floor. It was early in the morning, at least for a Saturday – 7am. I had to work on Saturdays. I had to work on Sundays, too; I worked every day other than Friday. The elevator again dinged again as the doors slid open. I put my head down and paced hurriedly out of the building.

From the lobby, I heard a familiar voice. I looked up. It was the housekeeping lady. She always wanted to make small talk with me.

"Dobroe Utro!" she said jovially. She was one of the few cheery people in the country. That was one of the things I loved about Russia – nobody gave a shit about people they didn't know; about people they weren't close with. I respected that. It spoke positively to my intense introversion. This old babushka was the exception to that rule. She was abnormally friendly.

I lifted my head halfway, nodding in her direction.

"Kak dela?" she continued.

"Horror show," I responded. I pressed the circular magnet of my key into the corresponding place in the thick, steel door, then pushing it ajar, pressing onward, against the wind, out into the dark, snowy cold of the morning.

It was windy. A shifting, powdery mist swayed against the cracked concrete of the sidewalk. The narrow street – crammed claustrophobically on either side with stuck, parked cars – led out from my Soviet-styled apartment building to the bustling highway, Rublevskoe Shosse. Six-foot-tall piles of plowed snow stood mountainous at every corner. Moscow never slept. It wasn't always very exciting – especially in this dense, bland section of the inner city – but it was nonetheless awake.

Green and yellow painted sidewalks and railings lined the path from the exit of my apartment around the bend of the building. I always wondered why the city chose to color all its public spaces green and yellow; it was such a shock to me – I expected red and blue. Green is the color of nature; green is the color of God. Yellow is… easily detected by people with poor vision? That's the logic, according to the city government.

A green and yellow, ten-foot fence separated my apartment building from the adjacent schoolyard – which housed a currently vacant playground; its plastic slides and swings sitting in dark, snowy abandonment.

They would soon be populated by screaming, crazed children, waddling through the snow in their thick jackets and woolen scarves – like that kid from A Christmas Story.

I trudged forward, stopping into the small Produkti shop in front of my building. It was a cavernous place, its wet, muddy floors lined with cardboard aisles – paths leading shoppers around each of the shelves, allowing one the opportunity to maintain dry feet, and keep the floor at least relatively clean. I walked directly to the front counter:

"Odin shawarma," I said.

I ate shawarma for breakfast, which most of my other western colleagues found disgusting. Hell, most Russian people found it disgusting, too. But shawarma is such a perfect food – I could never help it. Especially shawarma in Russia. The best shawarma in the world is crafted in Russia. You may be thinking that I'm crazy, but it's true. Russian shawarma combines the best of both Turkish and Soviet cultures. Immigrants from Azerbaijan, or Turkmenistan, or Uzbekistan, move to Moscow and open shawarma shops, or streetside food stands. The chicken is still cooked and seasoned on a spit, in classic Mediterranean style, but in Moscow, there are added Russian ingredients. The tzatziki sauce is thick, with a hint of Russian garlic and mayonnaise. Dill is sprinkled all over the wrap. This creamy, Georgian brand of hot sauce – which I've never seen outside of the former Soviet world, is doused heartily, streaking across the top of the wrap. Sometimes, you could get the chicken doused in ajika. The combined ingredients are wrapped in lavash rather than pita. You can wash the whole thing down with some kvass. It's somehow perfect while trudging through the snow. It can make you sick, sometimes, though – if you catch the wrong stand. Shawarma stands are becoming a thing of the past, though – at least to some extent; it seems Putin doesn't like them. That was always one of my biggest worries, in Russia – the disappearance of shawarma.

Anyway, it was my usual breakfast.

I had to walk under the highway to get to school. In Russia, most highways house in their underbelly a walking path through which pedestrians can easily traverse. Upon witnessing this engineering success for the first time, I wondered why every highway didn't have – as a standard procedure upon construction – walking paths beneath them. I'm still not sure why. Maybe because we hate walking, in America.

Underneath the highways exists bustling life – shopkeepers selling clothes, or coffee, or booze; hawkers trying to hustle unwitting passersby; buskers playing music. It's really an interesting culture, under there. The highway near my apartment building, however – considering its location in the densely residential inner city, featured nothing so interesting. There was one guy that played guitar, though. He opened his case and set it out in front of him, in classic busker fashion, as he played his tunes. The music sprang off the walls of the tunnel, giving it a strong reverb. I liked that. He played some songs I recognized; he always played Zombie by The Cranberries. That song is popular in Russia – I'm not sure whether for political reasons or just because people like screaming zombie. He would sing that song often. That and Nirvana stuff. Say it Ain't So, by Weezer. He couldn't speak English, but he had memorized the pronunciation. He sounded pretty good.

I didn't see him that morning, though – the tunnel was empty. I trudged through it, emerging from the depths on the other side of the highway – out into the courtyard of a block of tall, leaning, Soviet-styled apartment buildings. The apartment buildings in Moscow, as numerous and massive as they are, all look identically shitty. It's amazing, really. What's more incredible, though, are the insides of the places. I don't think I've ever gone into a Russian apartment that wasn't super nice – even the homes of poor families. The place is always clean, nice looking, and it always has a glittering chandelier hanging from the ceiling in the middle of the living room. Every Russian household requires a chandelier – it's a cultural tradition. It shows that you have more money than you need; you have cash to burn. The exterior of any Russian apartment building in no way reflects its interior. It's like walking into a different universe – a Russian Narnia. It's strange.

I pushed through the empty courtyard, which housed in its center a playground and an outdoor gym. Swings swung creaking in the soft morning wind. I threw the plastic bag formerly housing my shawarma in a green metal trash bin outside the entrance to one of the buildings. A stray cat, laying in front of the door to the apartment building, glanced up at me apathetically.

The snow continued. I put in my earbuds.

I love music. It detaches me from reality, and it also deters people from talking to me. I especially love it when I'm in a foreign country. I like finding the bands whose music I think fits the atmosphere of the place – in both the sense of the place's soul itself, and also in the sense of my subjective opinion of my surroundings.

Beach House and Fleet Foxes always seemed to fit in so well with Russia. Beach House sounds like snow; Fleet Foxes sound like medieval eastern Europe. At least to me.

I flipped through my iPod – I still had one of the classic models, with the spin wheel – and settled on Days of Candy, by Beach House. No song more than that one fits with a dark, depressing, snowy morning. If you have a hangover, it makes it somehow even more fitting.

I stood idly at the intersection, snow buffeting my face as I waited for the crosswalk light to change to green. Down the street a way, not far from where I stood, sat a small Orthodox chapel. It was a wooden building with a green, corrugated metal roof and a glittering, gold-colored onion-dome. A small wooden fence surrounded the building, protecting it from the numerous, surrounding Khrushchyovki apartment buildings, which had closed in on the small church like a pack of wolves greedily encircling a fawn. That's one the many interesting things about Russia. In no other place can you see the history of the place more clearly. It's right in front of your face, all the time. The contrast between the Rurik dynasty, the house of Romanov, the Soviet Union, and the Putin-era is everywhere apparent in the architecture. This distinction makes it easy to appreciate the culture and history.

I crossed the street. As I was walked, a Yandex Taxi speeding down the snowy road halted abruptly, sliding in front of the cross walk. Yandex is essentially the Russian version of Google and Uber, if those two companies were combined. I ignored it and pressed forward. That's the way traffic works, in Russia. You have to assume that speeding cars won't hit you. It's unnerving, at first, but you get used to it. Being a passenger in a Russian taxi is a bit of a different story, however; I never fully got used to that. I would always grip tightly the doorhandle and seat-cushion of the backseat, expecting at any moment to crash hard into another vehicle, or fly off the road.

I turned the corner into the courtyard housing the small school where I worked. I taught mostly Kindergarten kids. I was so terrible at it, for the longest time, but I had finally developed ability enough to consider myself a serviceable elementary teacher. The thing with kids, is you can't get flustered when your plans go to shit. If kids don't like something, they won't do it. It's as simple as that, so you can't expect to be any sort of disciplinarian when they won't do the shit you planned for them. The best strategy is to have a variety of activities at the ready and hope one of them catches the interest of the kids long enough to keep them busy for a full lesson. My Kindergarten lessons at this school were an hour and a half long, so keeping interest was often difficult. Lots of music, games, and crafts – that's what I found to be the most effective strategy. And the occasional Peppa Pig cartoon – Svinka Peppa is incredibly popular in Russia.

I twisted the key into the lock and opened the thick, steel door of the school. The happy, jangling alarm alerted the empty building my presence. The place was pitch-dark. Nobody liked working on the weekends, but all the parents wanted weekend English lessons for their kids – so the school had to operate. Some of my Russian coworkers would arrive a little later, whenever they woke up, but I was mainly looking for Bruce – an old British guy I was supposed to be training. Bruce had left his home in Birmingham because he was tired of his life in the UK. He wanted some adventure, so he decided to move to Russia. I can't say I was optimistic about his chances of becoming an effective English teacher.

I sat down at the bench in the foyer of the building, grabbing a couple light blue, plastic bags to wrap around my muddy shoes. I had forgotten to bring my indoor slippers, called tapochki, in Russia, so I had to use the bags. They seemed strange when I had first arrived, but they were necessary. Cars, sloshing through the snow, would color every sidewalk brown with gas and exhaust-flavored snow. There was no way to keep shoes clean, and – without the tapochki – no way to keep the inside of a building clean, either.

I stood and walked to the water cooler, grabbing a small, six-ounce plastic cup, dropping in a bag of Earl-Grey, and filling it with steaming hot water. Bobbing the bag up and down in the cup, I sipped the aromatic tea.

Bruce walked in a few moments later:

"Morning, you okay?" he said, waddling into the room, breathing heavily. Bruce had a bit of an odor about him, but I'm not sure he could help it. He was a large dude, and he was probably sixty years old; I'm sure it wasn't easy for him, trudging through snow-buried Moscow. He reached in his jeans pocket and pulled out a couple small packages of Nescafe instant coffee, which were labeled intense, I guess because they contained an extra caffeine kick. Bruce ripped one of the packages open and dumped it into his plastic cup:

"You want one?" he said, "I got this other one for you."

"Not right now," I responded, lifting my cup of tea, "I'll take you up on the offer after I finish this one off."

"Earl-Grey!" said Bruce, "My kind of lad!"
We went into the classroom, which was carpeted a shaggy, 80's-era pale green, and began setting up. I told Bruce that we needed to prepare our craft, cartoon, story, and game. We would intersperse these primary activities with music and dancing. That's how Kindergarten classes worked – that's the only way they would be successful. You had to be ready. Bruce swung open the large window, letting in a frigid morning breeze. You really do get used to the cold, in Russia. I didn't mind it at all – I was glad that Bruce opened the window. Something about crisp, wintry air is reenergizing.

"So, I'm going to let you read the story, and do the other activity you've prepared," I said.

Bruce was a teacher in training. He was mostly just participating in the class as an aid, but the management wanted him to lead a few activities on his own. I told hm I'd give him the story – being that reading a children's book is straightforward – and let him plan something of his own. If his planned activity didn't work out, it was no big deal – half of the activities anyone plans don't work out, in kindergarten classes.

"What story are you going to read?" I continued.

"This one, I think," said Bruce, removing There's a Wocket in my Pocket, by Dr. Suess, from the bookshelf as if grabbing something at random. He probably had, but it was a good choice. It's a classic story, that one.

"Great," I said, "And what are you going to do for your other activity?"

"I reckon I'm going to teach them how to count!" he said, "I'll take this whiteboard," he said, gesturing to the wooden tripod whiteboard sitting in the corner of the room, "and have them write numbers on it. Maybe I'll use the Wocket in the Pocket book, have them count hidden monsters around the room, and then have them write that number on the board. Maybe I'll use these magnets to make the shape of the number, and then have them trace it with a marker. We could even play monster hide-and-seek after that, if it's all right by you."

"That's a hell of an idea," I said, "You're really a natural at this, Bruce."

It was a good idea, but Bruce, unfortunately, wasn't a natural.

The children began arriving not long after that, the cheery, ringing bell continuously signaling their presence at the front door. After I let them in, their parents would sit and apply plastic bags to their feet. The children would run chaotically around the building, destroying anything entering their line of sights like chimpanzees freed from enslavement at the zoo.

"All right, all right!" I yelled, shepherding them into the classroom, "It's time to begin our English lesson!"

I would smile at the parents before forcing closed the misaligned classroom door. They would smile back. Most of them weren't competent English speakers. They would occasionally say basic phrases, like "How are you?", or "Good morning!", or "Weather is bad!", and I would do the same to them in Russian, but for the most part, it was smiling and nodding.

I always closed the door to the classroom because teaching often gave me anxiety, which worsened if I knew anyone was watching me. I didn't even like having Bruce there, honestly, and he was about as carefree as a person can get. It didn't matter, anyway. The walls were paper-thin. The parents kept their ears perked; they listened to the entirety of every lesson. Some of them even literally put their ear to the door; I knew that because I accidentally rammed one of them once while pushing it open. It's a bizarre atmosphere, teaching Kindergarten in Russia.

Our lesson went over smoothly. We sang our introductory, morning songs and practiced our new vocabulary. I held out flash cards, featuring photos of different vehicles, and had the students parrot basic sentences back to me.

"It's a blue train!" I would say.

"It's a blue train!" They would repeat excitedly.

"Do you like trains?" I would say.

"Yes, I do!" they would answer, slapping their hands against their thighs to get the syllabic rhythm of the pronunciation.

I would give them a high-five, after that, assuming they actually said the phrases. Sometimes, I would retract my hand at the last moment, causing them to miss. They thought that shit was hilarious.

Bruce's portion of the lesson went over well, too. He read the Dr. Suess story, which was always a hit, and actually got some students to write numbers on the whiteboard. The hide-and-seek game was a bit of a mess, but that was to be expected. Before I knew it, we were singing our goodbye song, and the ninety minutes was finished.

Bruce worked up a sweat during the lesson, the heavy smell of which permeated the small classroom. I had to open the window; I didn't want the student's parents thinking I smelled like that. Upon swinging ajar the large window, the students – three or four of which always remained to play in the classroom after the lesson had finished – jumped onto the wide, plastic windowsill and began pointing outside, conversing in their childish vernacular. I enjoyed it when they did that; it was one of the best ways for me to learn Russian. Children use very simple vocabulary, and they scream almost everything they say, unlike adults, who have a tendency to mumble.

Vanya pointed out the window: "That's my mom's car!"

Ivan did the same: "And that's my mom's car!"

Sasha joined in: "Look! It's snowing!"

Alina did the same: "Look! That's a big tree!"

I felt proud when I understood those simple sentences.

Leaving the classroom, I dumped Bruce's intense coffee into my plastic cup, filling it at the water-cooler. The parents wanted me to give their students "homework", so after each lesson, I was expected to go over with them the vocabulary, phrases, and reading/writing skills we practiced during the lesson. I talked to them, downed my cup of coffee, removed the plastic from my shoes, put on my coat, and trudged back out into the snowy morning. After lunch, I would return for another class. After that, I would walk to the metro and travel across the city, where I had an evening private lesson with a kid at his house. That was my basic schedule. It was a lot of walking, and a lot of riding the metro. I enjoyed, though, for the most part. I would have hated it, if I'd had to do that in my hometown, but travelling around a foreign city, especially one as massive as Moscow, never completely dulled for me, even after I'd been doing it for three years.

I'd like to go back there, someday, but the current state of events in the world is unlikely to allow that of me, at least not for quite some time. I think I'm done teaching Kindergarten, though – I don't have the energy, or the patience, for it anymore.

PORTRAIT IN WATERCOLOR: THE INHABITANTS OF HOUSES

AVE JEANNE VENTRESCA | USA

below this geometry of geese, whose
wings of symmetry crosses
sky all chubby clouds, and within earth
of different shades of brown,
we build houses.

we fill them with bison hides and
reassuring old chairs, coneflowers, and
nights of dancing. to keep them resilient,
every wall owns its own pigment, each
floor contains a certain number of tears,
and intricate patterns of tradition. we give

them inhabitants. allow them dreaming
and anticipation. adorn them with hymns
for unforeseen directions. we call them by
name, pronounce each out loud when we
make love or share faces

with death. we speak
these names, light like feathers, on days
of importance. when throats are dry
and memories many. below these rooftops

we create
purposeful arrangements of adjectives and
nouns to make emotions noticeable to others.
we gather corn, bean, and conversations,
constantly aware how wind flows bold, and
seasons become full.

like large buffalo, we tend to together stand,
in graveyards where silence is the home.
now, relying on weeds and thick roots
to support our heavy skulls.

WHITE CARD

MIRA MOOKERJEE | ENGLAND

Farhad struggled to the front of the food queue. He knew there was not enough food for everyone and if he waited patiently at the back, they would choose to feed the cute kids instead of him. Farhad was only six, but everyone mistook him for older. He waved some crumpled papers at the woman handing out food to prove that he was in the process of getting a white card which would identify him as a registered asylum seeker.

"Food and juice," he commanded in English. A young girl standing behind him giggled.

"Come on now Farhad, you know you should say please," the charity worker replied, her eyebrows raised.

"Food and juice. Please." Farhad said, flashing his teeth.

"Aftó to paidí," the charity worker exclaimed in Greek, shaking her head, and handing him a tray, her plastic glove covered hand brushing against Farhad's bare skin. Her blue eyes watched in expectantly, "now what do you say Farhad?"

"Ef-ari-stó-polý ky-ri-a," Farhad replied, thanking her in overly syrupy Greek. He stuck out his tongue and darted away.

Farhad loved food, but the food they served at the camp was stodgy, salty, and bland. He used to make fun of the food with the other kids, but as his meals became fewer and further between, Farhad had started wolfing down his dinner in a quiet corner by himself. He finished his drink and tossed the empty containers into an overflowing bin.

Farhad made his way back to a corrugated iron structure, picking his way past a mass of temporary tents before locating his own. His older sister Zarina sat inside, washing his clothes in a plastic basin. He flopped an arm round her shoulder and kissed her cheek, causing water to spill on to the floor of their tent.

"Farhad! Ist!" she scolded him in Farsi. Farhad smiled back at her lovingly. She sighed and stroked his hair, "you get food and jimon?" she asked.

"Not jimon! Juice!" Farhad said, correcting her Greek to English,

"Juice, jimon, âbmive, same same," she said, "you get any?"

"Aare," Farhad responded, licking his lips.

"Any for me?" Zarina continued in Farsi.

Farhad looked down at the ground guiltily, he had been so hungry he had forgotten he was meant to save some for his sister.

"Farhad!" she said, whacking him over the head with a wet towel.

"Sorry, sister, sorry," Farhad said, his eyes fixed on the floor.

Zarina sighed and pushed a shoulder into Farhad, "go play," she ordered him, "you take up too much room."

Farhad left quickly and went on a hunt for his friends. On the other side of the camp, he could see a group of children playing. He wanted to join them, but it was on the side where all the PKK flags were, and his sister had told him it wasn't safe for the two sides of the camp to mix. Farhad didn't understand why. The children looked friendly, and that side of the camp didn't look any different from his side, but there were a lot of things Farhad had come to accept that he did not really understand. Farhad walked around until he found his friend Salim sitting on a wall. Salim was fourteen, the same age as Farhad's sister, but Farhad thought he was a lot more fun that Zarina.

"Ahlan Farhad!" Salim said, greeting him in Arabic, "kayf halik?"

"Ahlan!" Farhad responded happily, switching to Arabic to talk to his friend, "anā bekheīr, but you know, my sister's being a pain."

"What's happening?" Salim asked him, gesturing for him to come and sit next to him.

Farhad sat himself on the wall beside Salim and explained the situation "I said I would share my food with her, but I forgot and now she is mad at me."

Salim laughed, "I would be mad at you too little brother," he said.

"Yes, but she does not even need the food!" Farhad continued, "have you seen her? She is getting so fat!" He said, moving his hands to mimic a round belly, "and she will not leave the tent to get her own anymore!"

Salim put an arm around Farhad's shoulder and looked at him seriously, "Farhad, you must make sure your sister eats."

Farhad sighed; he knew Salim was right.

"Hey," said Salim, changing the subject, "I heard there might be new people arriving to the camp."

"Who?" said Farhad.

"People from Ukraine," explained Salim, "there is a war with Russia, so people are having to leave."

"A lot of people?" Farhad asked.

Salim nodded, "I think so."

Farhad wondered where there would be space for the Ukrainians to sleep in the camp, he hoped there would be enough tents for them. Maybe the camp would be made bigger, he thought. Farhad had heard of Russia, but he did not know where Ukraine was.

"What do they speak in Ukraine?" He asked Salim.

Salim shrugged, "I don't know."

"I hope it is Farsi," said Farhad.

Farhad had picked up a good amount of Arabic. Most of the kids around him spoke either Arabic or Dari, but he still missed some of the jokes and struggled to understand when everyone was talking over one another. He knew some Greek too, but Zarina had told Farhad that he must study English and German, as those were the countries they were hoping to settle in. Farhad didn't like English or German very much, he thought German sounded like someone trying to cut down a tree and English sounded like a lot of words without proper endings bumping into one another. Both languages were very harsh and hard. It would be nice, he thought, if these Ukrainians spoke Farsi like he did.

"Farhad, do you still have that football?" Salim asked, breaking Farhad's train of thought.

Farhad nodded.

"Go fetch it and we will play," said Salim.

Farhad ran back to his tent to find his ball and tell his sister the news about the new arrivals from Ukraine.

"It means there will be more people coming to the camp," he told her as he rummaged around their tent.

Zarina shook her head, "they will not come here," she said.

Farhad stopped looking for his ball and looked at her, "why not?" he asked.

"I have seen them in Athens already," Zarina explained, "they do not need papers or white cards to get support like we do."

"But why?" Farhad asked, assuming he was missing something, "are they not also refugees like we are?"

"Yes, they are also refugees." Zarina responded.

Farhad thought for a moment, but he was still confused, "is the war in Ukraine worse than other wars? Are they in more danger than we are?"

Zarina shook her head, "war everywhere is bad. We are all in danger."

Farhad paused, "so why do we need to wait for white cards and papers?"

Zarina looked into her brother's young eyes and decided to change the subject, "what are you looking for little brother?"

"My ball," he replied, "but I don't think it is here anymore."

"No matter," she said, "it is getting dark so you should sleep now anyway," Farhad stuck out his bottom lip, "but," Zarina continued, sensing her brother's frustration, "next time I go to Athens I will find you a new ball."

Farhad smiled and nodded his head, "will you work in Athens tonight?" he asked.

"No, no, not tonight," Zarina replied.

"Okay," said Farhad, "I like it better when you stay here anyway."

Zarina smiled and stroked her little brother's head, "go to sleep now."

Farhad wriggled into his sleeping bag and closed his eyes. He had grown used to the noise around him and he soon fell asleep.

In Farhad's dream he was back in with his mother, his head in her lap. He could hear her singing his favourite lullaby and could smell oranges on the trees outside. He struggled to keep his eyes open, watching the white curtains that framed a view of the mountains sway in the breeze. He could hear the rustle of papers coming from his father's study next door. He wondered if he had time to kiss his father goodnight before he fell asleep. He wanted to ask his mother, but his body was so tired. With effort, he turned his head to hers and focused his eyes on her face. But what he saw was a blur, a mash of smudged colours without any identifiable features. Farhad was frightened, what had happened to his mother? He tried to reach out to her, but he could not. She was no longer singing, and Farhad could feel water dripping on his face. His mother was fading, her body floating away from him, her arms swaying limply like the curtains in his bedroom.

Farhad woke to realise his throat was sore from screaming. He blinked until the green walls of his tent came back into focus. His sister's arms were wrapped round him, rocking him against her swollen belly.

"It's okay Farhad," she soothed him, "you're okay. I'm here, I'm here."

AN ORPHANED CLOTHESLINE

DEBASISH MISHRA | INDIA

When bodies cease to exist
their relics cling to clothes

the smell of skin and the music
of voices lost in a babble

The clothes know the secrets
of the bodies like mirrors

where there was a mole
where there was a sore

The clothesline admits the secrets
and resets to a tabula rasa

the dance of democracy
to the tunes of the breeze

where every cloth gets
an equal share of the sun

where everything is cleaned
every organ is cleansed

but the clothesline can't forget
the brown hands that blistered

with washing powder and left
the clothes to dry between

the wall and the sun like
a variegated streak of streamers

Those hands won't come again
to take these clothes home

SELF-PORTRAIT WITH XYLEM

JOSHUA EFFIONG | NIGERIA

What do you make of a boy whose framework was fashioned by all the women in him? Here, I'm in my mother's womb, & it's delivery day. Contraction shreds her uterine muscle fibers as my grandmother nudges & soothes her to push me into her open arms. Mother fix her gaze in the hole on the thatched roof over her head. Today, the sun is in its full glory. A scream escapes my mother's lip as she takes a deep breathe & I slither out of her. At evening, my umbilical cord is prayed upon, & buried beside the grave of my late grandfather while I nap in my mother's arm with a body properly scrubbed & smeared with kernel oil to dispel every evil meted against me. After this pattern of modeling, what will be the mechanics of my being? Sincerely, I bear in me the genealogy of women. Of half-baked literacy. Of poverty. & every time my faith shrinks, I practice rebaptism in the oasis of memories flourishing in me.

BEFORE WINDMILL HILL

OLIVER SMITH | ENGLAND

Like a gull blown westering from the sea,
an immigrant, too-recently stranded
to yet belong, made fall. She sang and danced
upon an alien shore. Her pale feet
made beginnings and she kindled a fire
on the cold sands, to cook an oyster stew;

the recipe passed down from mouth to mouth;
a hundred ages, with a word for each
river, each green plant, each fantastic fruit,
each mountain. She named hearth and flower.
In the vale, she named home. She named hives
and crops and goats and kine. She named children

so they might be held like meat and milk
on her tongue; like music and love, like wheat
and honey. She stained her lips with memory
and her mouth smiled sweet with joy.
She danced upon the green hills, raised a stone
to guide her folk on the smooth chalk downs

above a serpent-river, where old gods swam,

slow and broad with moonlight. Downstream,

under the northern stars, she dug shallow

for crops, deep to rest the hearts of lovers

who dreamt with her of icy waves and held

her still, in dreams, lost in the years and days.

She found an end; stretched deep her roots and slept

cupped in the bowl of an oak. The tree curled

like an old woman's tired fingers. Held her

as one native to the work of land and time.

She renamed herself soil and bone and lay

fire stained from the kiln; earth stained from the clay.

RED

DMT | SOUTH AFRICA

i am queer because

    a. i didn't survive into straightness

    b. my mother was a breadwinner

    c. i'm funny that way, ha ha

    d. i went off the path and the forest took me for a wolf

it is sad because

    a. god says no

    b. the forest is scary

    c. i howl with a human voice

    d. the humans had sown rocks into their stomachs, convinced that nature is best consumed, that forests are fires waiting to happen

i left my church because

    a. my, what big eyes i had

    b. my, what big paws i had

    c. how sharp my teeth when

    d. the body is bread

red riding hood was

    a. a screaming child

    b. god's blessing to man-kind

    c. the future, a womb that carried a basket of sweets

    d. a necessary sacrifice, to the elderly

and so
with their pitchforks they came
with their leashes and cages
with their bibles, for ages
into the forest
as god watched

god, the birds in the trees as axes swung
and smoke rose,
an offering to the sky that only clouds could taste

HEADLESS

NWUGURU CHIDIEBERE SULLIVAN | NIGERIA

Have we not come near enough like hair,
like blood, like sweat to the six decades

of this skin? Wasn't enough ball of sun lost
to the gluttony of this land brimming with

yawning graves? Have we forgotten how the
limbs of a man are quadrupled to a god exercising

his powers from the four cardinal points? Here,
all we know is how the zings of bullets eat

a chimney into what is wet & fleshy, so that
it may have enough proteins to ease off

the wrestling rain from every tired cloud.
The bullets here, measure the depth of one's

flesh by swimming through the dirt of blood
& still, come out clean & bare like a pure

conscience. My Twitter is scared to warm-boot,
says the government laid a cold ban on it & I'm

full-throated with grief for myself who came out
of a bright syntax to morph a phrase into a sentence,

forgetting that every word is a conglomerate of
letters which once knew independence. A country

is a bordered sentence— it doesn't permit winging,
it abhors flight, which is why it forces the stony

hands of each day down our throats as templates
of laws, which is why it takes our head first,

leaving us to live the rest of our lives headless—
hopeless. O ample— O bold— O blunt & blue,

how come my shine ages as it
passes through you?

BREAKING DOWN

MEENAKSHI BHATT | INDIA

Not long ago, my husband and I were about to go on a morning walk. The sky was overcast with clouds. The rain seemed imminent. However, we told ourselves, "We don't intend to go far. It looks like we still have a few minutes of dry weather left". We were wrong.

The wind started blowing furiously just as we stepped out into the open. Next came the rain. We retreated to the safety of our apartment complex. The stairs in our apartment complex are partially shielded from the elements and afford a clear view of the outside. We sat on the stairs and watched the wind perform it's frenzied dance.

The wind whipped the trees around. The branches of some trees broke and some others came perilously close to losing a part of their foliage. In the sky, the clouds blew past at an unusually rapid rate. Sitting where we were, we were not in danger but the gods were certainly making themselves visible and audible. That experience got me thinking about the way nature does its housekeeping. Things that get too big to be managed are broken down to a manageable size, time and time again.

Why doesn't nature endow us, humans, with the same capacity to intermittently shed our excessive burdens? Why are we obsessed with incessant growth and constant productivity?

It is not nature that is to blame.

We, too, get tired of the daily grind. We, too, get exhausted from jobs that appear repetitive and meaningless. We have just lost the ability to pick up these cues.

All our lives we have been swamped by messages that exhort us to keep going at any cost. We have been told we can do anything if we try hard enough. In this modern way of living, there is neither the time nor the inclination to listen to the voice of nature.

We work even when we are tired. We use stimulants to stay awake far longer than our body would allow us. We eat beyond fullness. We exercise despite the pain. We continue to remain in jobs and relationships that make us feel unsafe and exhausted.

Similarly, the systems we live in and work in refuse to heed the signs of overload. The productivity that is expected of us is often beyond human physical capacity. Even when it is physically achievable, our minds are incapable of all the cognitive load that is heaped upon us. This unnatural exhaustion is then termed burnout. Vacations, meditation, mindfulness, and medications are advised as solutions when the only logical solution is to stop making unnatural demands of people.

When individuals and systems stretch themselves beyond the breaking point, they break. It is natural. It is time to slow down and notice the hints that nature keeps giving us. It is time to do regular course corrections, if not at the systemic level, then at least at the individual level. It is time to opt out of lifestyles and situations that demand perpetual superhuman effort from us.

SNOWFLAKES OF YESTERDAY

SAM SAFAVI-ABBASI | IRAN & UNITED STATES

snowflakes of yesterday,
slowly forming, dancing, reaching,
gathering together.
into a veil of white
covering trees, stones, lakes
surfacing everything.
then, melting with the sun-
with a veil of white remaining,
the veil of memories-
the coverings of yesterday.

today a soldier died.
today, someone's son, a daughter.
today, someone's blood,
under the unborn blossoms-
today, the trees.

today, someone's salty tears.
today, the hands of violence.
today, we care for your grandmothers.
yesterday, you killed our daughters.

yesterday, the snow, the cold shivering lips.
today was the brothers' birthday.
today someone without identity.
today I cry.
yesterday the snow was white.
yesterday the snow.

yesterday 'Power' tricked you again.
today your truth was weaponized.
yesterday you missed the snow.
yesterday 'Power' tricked you again.
yesterday the snowflakes couldn't lie.
yesterday the snow.
the snowflakes of yesterday are now gone.

THE WORLD THAT LOVED EXECUTIONERS

VYACHESLAV KONOVAL | ENGLAND

Grain in the throat,

like a trading card,

playing a game,

it seems that the «players»

fragile the bureaucrats,

their voters chew healthy cereal.

Western leaders love gifts,

big bonuses, pay for cynicism,

it's easy to wrap the ice cream

naming grief as «comprehensive pluralism».

How easy it is to tire of violence,

forget about your «concern»,

deep in the executioner's arms,

Guterres said to Putin: «I love you».

It doesn't matter what your state is,

look at the map

everything is conditional

radiation will be carried by the winds,

and the warm sea will bring.

A COUNTRY OF BONE & MEDIEVAL ROT

NNADI SAMUEL | NIGERIA

A country's banner swallowed us whole,
& the wailing of a child tears through the border of language.
at a sacristy in Vietnam, a mother witnesses a wooden seraph
shapeshift under the dim light, & pandemonium ravages her loin
for this carved statue of the Colonists.

a Catechist in a bloodied cassock, tongues a homily in a Hebrew accent,
on a plundered field turned to wasteland.
a hand shreds through the ribs of my imagination
& fashions a toy boat named exile:

this phrase, washes my lineage ashore.
the bane of a roaming corpse that renders us homeless.
tonight, the country's vagabonds—all blade scholars, press their lips
to the ground & howl into wetness, until breathless,
hoping, the land softens at the mention of grief.

a thug empties his fist into a Kalashnikov.
in the year of slavery & nailed barracoons, palace guards lay in
a plank pose—reciting newer ways to die.
It's a fated curse, the way one generation lives to enslave the next.

each household, enduring with the absence of a male—
freshly eaten by a conflict. city of bone & medieval rot.

in a shallow plantation, a woman debones her child to fit into a casket.
"this war won't outlive our lineage" she whispers.

an uproar of dead relatives, tearing through dust.
my father turns in his grave.
"Lord, how many headstones make a cementery?"

a vulture soars over a skull,
towards the low-hanging cloud—chewed by vitiligo.
the emptiness is a torment, with sky eaten to the ground.
here, the origin of my exile.

BOYS OF THE SAVANNA

CHINEDU GOSPEL | NIGERIA

There's a God. And there are
voices that whir from beneath

    the turf — angels, ancestors. Our boys

are buried under the grass. Because
where I'm from, they'd grow into a

    forest of trees — evergreen, beautiful, godly.

There's a boy. And there are arrows
& bullets searching for home between

    his ribs. There's a woman, a mother tired

of asking God for opened doors in her
prayers. Because at the doorway of every

    open door there was a bullet aimed at her

son's skull, for being young. & being
green. & being Nigerian. This is the

    story of the Savanna; there's a sheep

on one end of the land. And a trigger-happy
shepherd on the opposite end. One

    inching closer towards the other is a bad omen.

The birds sing it. The cloud with
gloom on its face sees it and cries.

    But, too blind, we do not see the ruin ripening.

MR. CARTER'S WOMEN

ANANDA KUMAR | INDIA

On Sunday evenings, Amma and I took the Activa to visit my maternal grandmother, Subha Paati's, and my great-grandfather in their Chennai home.

Subha Paati said her father loved the United States much more than the three wives and seventeen children he left behind in Madras, as he traveled to New York through safe delivery system of the Luce-Celler Act. As Brooklyn unraveled before his eyes, he changed his name to Michael Carter, married his lactose intolerant landlady, poisoned her cat, and bought a tobacco shop in Fulton Street from a man of Parsi origin who was secretly leaving his five motherless children to go to Paris and learn the violin.

In 2019, Mr. Carter learned that he had stage-four bladder cancer.

"But it is unfortunate," Subha Paati added, "that things turn out to be fine and peachy for shifty old men like him. No matter how bad and irresponsible they have been, no matter how abusive, their family always takes care of them." His now-fifty-year old American-landlady-bride turned out to be so fertile that she gave him seven daughters. And those seven daughters married seven young men (all of them white, protestant and non-smokers). And they all gave him twenty-five grandchildren.

Of his many grandchildren, only one, Linda, truly cared for sick Mr. Carter and thought it a great idea to send him back to Chennai, to Subha Paati, one of Mr. Carter's daughters from his second marriage. Linda said she'd take care of his medical expenses and all my grandmother had to do was look after him.

"Wow, aren't you the generous foreigner!" Subha Paati said to her on her Zoom call. "Sending him back to us, just so he wouldn't stink up your fancy corner of the world!"

Linda never contacted us again. The third of every month, money comes into Subha Paati's bank account, and she spends the money lavishly on herself.

Subha Patti was born the day before Mr. Carter left her mother in 1950. Everyone blamed Subha Paati for driving her father away from her mother. Her mother descended into melancholia: postpartum was another silly excuse for women to not work and so people thought she was just being difficult. Subha Paati's mother didn't eat or sleep or talk for days, refusing even to feed her daughter.

When Subha Paati turned fifteen, her mother confessed to something: that she was taking a bath in the river, and had suddenly felt an unknown gaping hole develop in her chest, and seeing water all around her, she let herself go, letting the current take her, thinking that would fill the hole. Refusing to swim for several minutes as the waves took her, she suddenly came back to her senses and reached the banks after much struggle.

My grandmother was deeply affected by her mother's confession. How could her mother think of leaving her, just as Mr. Carter left their family behind? At a very small age, Subha Paati understood that adults get to act reckless with impunity, and that children are the victims. So she decided she had to grow up faster because being a child doesn't help. And for a start, she wanted to make some money for herself so as to afford to live on her own in the city and go to college. She knew that Mr. Perkins, the neighbourhood Anglo-Indian pianist could help, as he had friends in high places in Madras; and so she asked him if she could be his maid. He happily obliged, and after school, she went to Mr. Perkins' house, where she made him his evening tea, baked him his rum cakes, made him his gin and tonic, cooked him his dinners, and also kept house for him.

On Sundays, when she would spend the whole day at Mr. Perkins' house, she would stop stirring his stew or mopping his floors or doing his dishes to instead listen to him play. She observed him writing symbols on a sheet of paper. Soon the compositions were etched in her mind, and she started seeing the correlating pattern of the notes and the symbols on the stave and sounds she heard when Mr. Perkins played.

Two months into the job, Mr. Perkins came home late one evening and found Subha Paati, studying the sheets of a Tchaikovsky piece he was playing the previous day. Sensing his presence in the room, Subha Paati dashed out and waited in the kitchen for Mr. Perkins to dismiss her for the day. In a few minutes he summoned her. She found him sitting at the piano; on the table where he took his evening tea, there was a blank music sheet and a pencil. She knew what was expected of her. He started playing a bit of Beethoven's Pastorale he arranged for the piano. In a few minutes he stopped, turned around and looked at Subha Paati expectantly.

With deliberation and deep thought, she took the pencil and started writing on the stave. She looked up at him when she was done with the notation for the part he played, and he walked up to her slowly, took the sheet and studied it in disbelief. Astonished by his fifteen-year old maid's ear for notation, he asked her whether she had experience transcribing before; to which she said that, to her, the whole thing looked like someone threw a bunch of crazy symbols at a precarious spider web. He then asked her whether she could play if he gave her a sheet to follow; and she said, sounding bashful and yet a little conceited: "I don't think I need this sheet, Mr. Perkins."

That's how Mr. Perkins, and later the world, came to know that my Subha Paati had music in her soul. Mr. Perkins used his every connection to earn her entry into Trinity College and soon she travelled all over the world, moving closely with legends like Martha Argerich, Janet Baker, and John Barbarolli.

Things turned out well for her, but she hasn't forgiven her parents. Though we call him Mr. Carter, to my grandmother, as long as he lies there on her rotten old bed riddled with bedbugs, in her care, the senile and sick absentee father is just a shifty absentee father.

Unlike, Subha Paati, Amma and I both treated Mr. Carter like any other human being. He had a soft spot for Amma because it is said she is the spitting image of my great-grandmother, which makes it easier for Subha Paati to stronghold a grudge against my mother. Amma said that she was used to it, that ever since she was a little girl, my grandmother had been holding her daughter's uncanny resemblance to her own mother against her.

"Whatever I did wasn't good enough," Amma shared with me. Once when Amma came second in long jump when she was eleven, Subha Paati scoffed and muttered, "No wonder you fell short!" When Amma was bedridden by chicken pox, Subha Paati blamed her for spreading it to Murthy uncle, Amma's younger brother, muttering: "You can't help it, can you?" When Amma was given a medal by the principal for not skipping school for even a day in eleventh standard, all Subha Paati had to say was: "Some medal for doing one's duty!" When relatives and well-wishers remarked that Amma looked like my great-grandmother, the former scoffed and said: "Let's hope she doesn't turn out to be useless as her as well."

The only time Amma ever felt she was worth something was when she met my father in college. He made her feel she was the center of his universe. My grandmother didn't approve of the match, so my mother eloped. I was born a year later, and Subha Paati came to visit in the hospital. My mother said she was standing a few feet away from the cradle and saw my father come in and take me in his arms. And one look at my father holding me, sitting beside Amma who was lying on the bed, the two of them sharing a quiet moment of admiration for the thing they created out of love—Subha Paati stormed out of the room, without a word. My father said the window in our hospital room had a view of the parking lot, and that he saw Subha Paati leaning against the hood of her car, her face buried in her palms, her body shaking from head to toe, trying so hard to keep it together.

The way Mr. Carter talked to Amma with such tenderness, the way he asked her to stay behind to complain about Subha Paati, the way he always wanted to hear her sing (as musical talent runs in the family, my mother's voice is divine), the way he always asked timidly to feed him dinner—all the attention he gave Amma was so foreign and gratifying to her that she failed to see how much he was hurting Subha Paati in the process and that it was his way of getting back at his daughter for the way he was being treated.

Sometimes Mr. Carter would ask me about my paintings. He asked me to sketch him once; and while I sat there, conjuring his image on paper, I was reminded of the audacious tale of a fifteen-year old Casanova for a father and his three marriages in India and the one in America. I remembered that when Subha Paati was finished with the tale, the first thing that came to my mind was: how on earth did he convince four separate women to marry and bare twenty-four children for him?

But, like they say how a question answers itself, it made sense to me: the way he made Amma feel on our visits, and how proud Subha Paati was for being the only child in all the twenty-four to fulfil her filial duty (for believe it or not, the Hindu version of Heaven is not outside her gamut, and Mr. Carter made her feel better every day with a promising place in it), it was no secret that he could play any woman like a fiddle.

And yes, Mr. Carter took us for granted. He thought my grandmother who took care of him, and my mother and I who came to visit him on Sundays and public holidays were—I believe the right word is—non-essential to the quality of his existence. Why? Because we were always around, and he believed we'll always be. My grandmother wouldn't starve him to death fearing damnation. My mother and I wouldn't hold what he did to Subha Paati against him because we were raised better.

I remember one Sunday when my father came to pick us up because my mother's twenty year old Activa's engine finally gave up and ceased. He came in to visit Mr. Carter, and the old man was ecstatic to finally meet someone with whom he can talk politics, cricket and how feminism is the new fascism.

They were inseparable for two hours, and when it was time for us to leave, to my utter astonishment, I saw Mr. Carter's eyes well up.

He said, with violent fits of sobbing choking him from time to time, that he had been such a fool to abandon his loving third wife (my great-grandmother was his second wife) and his infant daughter to run off to America. I still remember my father's words that were meant to console him: "Now, now, Mr. Carter, you shouldn't worry. Look at them. Your girls all turned out to be great. Your daughter is a prodigy, your granddaughter is a leading virologist, and your great-granddaughter is a Picasso in the making. Look at these girls. Look at what you have made, Mr. Carter!"

SKIN TOO THICK

FADRIAN ADRIAN BARTLEY | JAMAICA

let us hold men in our hands to feel their rough edges between our fingers,

and massage their temper before we misunderstand.
let us submit our attention
and allow the moment to breathe,
so their inner voice will speak through puffing cigars.
let us speak to them in silence

let them know that giants cannot crush the rain with bare hands.
or sweep away the river with their lashes.
let them feel comfortable to empty their soul
and release the clogged tunnel in their veins,
let them know that petals bleed when no one is looking.

RIPPLING SONG OF SCARS

CHINECHEREM ENUJIOKE | NIGERIA

my therapist warns that my hate will consume me/so, i begin from childhood may the grief of my innocence bear me witness/i write from the chords of an eight-year-old/one who knew voices that did not speak/one who knew hands whose coarseness ripped her off her innocence/she had watched the blue sky and saw it grey/she had sought the rains and each time they came/the drops brought dust/the one that tastes like the brown of rusted zinc/i write from the chords of an eighteen-year-old/who after ten years still sees dreams/each night begging the cosmos for amnesia/where i am/there are no ripples in the water/the calm intrigues me/i put my feet in the calm stream/ and forget how still waters run deep/that its depth may take my dreams away/and like God/breathe in me anew/that where my faith fails/fate may be on hold or do its worst/that, is the only way i can have amnesia/and not forget the face of my mother/i write from the chords of a mother/whose voice is an octave that leaves cracks in pillars and walls/like the stroke of koboko on the succulent bum of a maiden/each crack with a scar/each scar with a story/of how hands that broke her walls live free from bars/my mother tells me to be patient/that all troubled waters will calm/that even shards of a broken mirror are all mirrors/so, the night i heard that his cerebrospinal fluid had gorged the thirst of the lustered tars i became/when he breathed his last/i took my first/fifty years of terror breaks now/she greys into her scars/she fades like the dream i no longer have.

SIMPLE OPERATIONS

ELAINE GAO | CHINA & USA (YOUTH)

One plus one equals two.
Black hair plus yellow skin equals Chinese,
who take your orange chicken order
and owns the best massage parlor.
But there's no place else for your forehead's crease.

One minus one equals zero.
Pretty Asian girl minus awful English equals a no.
They own the classroom's corners,
the farthest ends of the bleachers.
Your lips curl in scorn as the referee calls go.

One times one equals one.
High IQ times good attitude equals A-student,
who monopolize rankings by teachers,
and modestly destroys white contesters.
But you only care that their social language isn't fluent

One divided by one is still one.
Your ego divided by their brilliance yields your ego.
They are thieves springing out of nowhere,
Robbing green bucks out of the rightful heirs
Your balled fists accompany a grunt.

AMALGAMATION

ALI ASHHAR | INDIA

Beneath the far horizon there's a ground;
beyond propaganda and prejudice,
between rain and sunshine,
where we assemble under the sky of art.
The rainbow portrays seven different shades
the sky knows—
all shades must come together
to make the world a splendid landscape.

IF WALLS COULD TALK

KALI FOX-JIRGL | USA

"SOMETIMES OUR WALLS EXIST JUST TO SEE WHO HAS THE STRENGTH TO KNOCK THEM DOWN"

If these walls could talk, my story may finally be heard. He killed me here — right here — but I am still very much alive. If these walls could talk, the justice of truth may set me free.

"Do you remember when I appeared to you as a prison wall?" I heard from seemingly nowhere as I hammered a nail into the wall. I looked around, but as I thought, there was no one else there, so I raised my hammer for one final blow.

"I said, do you remember when I appeared to you as a prison wall?" There it was again. The voice sounded old and distinct, but I couldn't place any recognition of it. "You're doing a fabulous job working through some heavy shit, young lady, and your decorating skills are top-notch, I love this shade of brown you have given me. The nails hurt a little, but I like the new art you're hanging on me. It's inspiring"

I looked down at the rustic wall hanging that I had just purchased.

NOTHING EVER GOES AWAY UNTIL IT TEACHES US WHAT WE NEED TO KNOW

— it read in stark white letters contrasting the dark wood the quote was painted on.

"I thought it was inspiring too", I said out loud as I hung it on my nail while trying to discern if my wall was actually talking to me. I straightened my newly hung piece of art and stood back to admire it. If my wall WAS talking, it was right, the message was inspiring. "What I need to know is why my wall is talking to me", I said out loud once more. I was kind of amused, and simultaneously considering I was losing my mind.

"You're an inspiration seeker. You look for the bigger meaning in everything. You search endlessly for answers to life's biggest questions", it said, "so let me ask you one more time, do you remember when I appeared to you as prison walls"?

As if I could ever forget thelife — the walls — that once held me hostage between them, stuck and scared for years. I was free to physically leave these walls whenever I wanted, I had a busy and zestful life on the other side of them, but when I was home, they were my subjective confinement.

"Yes, of course, I remember", I replied solemnly. He killed me here.

"I have been here, steady, and bearing the weight of structure for over 75 years, my dear. I have witnessed a tremendous amount of human conduct and social graces throughout my time…

I hated these walls again at this moment. What they were implying. I knew I had been horribly mistreated by my husband, but I was keeping that oppression in the past where it belonged and where I finally put him just the same. I kept this house in the divorce and had redecorated, so to speak, giving them a fresh coat of positivity and transformative anticipation of walls with no metaphoric bars.

"You didn't answer my question." the wall said to me after a long moment of silence.

"Sorry, I got lost in thought", I replied and confirmed the answer to the question.

"I know you did, I see you do it all the time, getting lost in your thoughts. You stare blankly at me, nearly catatonic at times, yet I can hear your heart beating at an alarming rate while you struggle to hold back tears", it said.

I must be truly insane, I thought to myself. Not only do I hear my walls talk, but I'm also engaging in discourse… with a wall! I needed a smoke, so I slid my slides on to go outside.

"Walls have ears, you know. I'm sure you've heard that before. Just watch out for the doors, they have eyes."

"What the hell, now you're a funny wall?", I retorted as I made my way to the front door with a sneer making sure it wasn't watching me.

"I have my moments. Comic relief is good sometimes. Wouldn't you agree? Not to be a bearer of bad tidings, but my ears are very acute, so when you sit outside and smoke your problems away, I can still hear everything. I rolled my eyes and threw up my hood to go have my problem-solving puffs.

"Make yourself a cup of coffee", my wall told me when I came back inside. "I have some little nuggets of wisdom to share with you. You're not going mad, doll", it continued, "you have burdened yourself long enough and it's time to let go."

As I started up my Keurig and added the hazelnut creamer my dad and I both had an infinity for; my heart missed him so much. He was my wisdom giver. As if my thought was spoken out loud, my wall, stoic like dad, said, "Your father told you once that you were the strong one in the family and I have seen that strength. It's remarkable, but you have to remember that fragility and vulnerability are a part of being human."

I sat down, holding my coffee mug in both hands as my Grandma used to, wondering if it was the warmth of the cup that comforted me or the memory of her. "I'm all ears", I said facetiously with a snicker, "comic relief."

"I see what you did there, good one," my wall laughed. "I remember the first time you walked through this house. A new state, new town, new beginnings. The first thing you wanted to do

was knock me down. Open things up. You were hopeful as you held your infant girl and watched your young boy run through with curiosity. He was the reason you were eager to get settled in and begin your new life here. It was his new chapter and you wanted to make sure it started on the right page. You built a solid foundation for him to start kindergarten in a good neighborhood full of families with children with whom he could make friends. You were devoted to being a mother regardless of how broken your marriage already felt. I know you wanted to leave him and I also know how difficult it was to leave your family to come here, but you had conquered everything in life thus far and knew you would conquer this transition too. As you made these walls your home, you were poised and tenacious with a vigor for life and that self-reliant courage you had always maintained."

It was right, my wall. I remembered that me.

"You and your son made friends rapidly and you adapted to small-town life even though you never thought you would be content in a place as trifling as this."

"I have adapted to every change, big or small, good or bad, in my life. I've always considered that one of my strengths," I replied.

"Yes, you have. You're very resilient, or, at least you used to be. I watched you degenerate slowly, though you never seemed to notice it was happening and you became powerless to stop it. The hypothetical demons that you had continuously and triumphantly quarreled with were taking new forms fueled by manipulation, intimidation, and aggression. Only by that horrific and invisible force did your mental armor begin to crack leaving you susceptible and weak to further blows from him. You see, his entire goal in life was to control and have power over others because it was he who was weak. A strong woman was never meant for his type, so he felt the only way to control you was through threats, malicious words, and a slow process of breaking down everything that made you who you were."

"Yeah, fuck him," I intentionally thought out loud this time. It had taken me nearly two years to stop the panic I felt just from seeing his name pop up on my phone wondering what spiteful and egotistical shit would erupt from his contentious mouth. He was the king of verbal vomit and it was always laced with lies to influence and control. He was always right, you know, and blameless in every situation. The compassionless, self-centered bastard who used to tell me I had fucked up morals while he defiled the very foundation of moral behavior.

He was an antagonist to the core of his being and the cause of my cynicism.

"Your pain didn't come from the bruises on your body... the wounds are far deeper than that. They are in your heart and scars on your mind. You cannot judge yourself by what others have done to you. Only you know your real self and what motivates you to continue this journey no matter how neglected the path may be. Your vital force has been tortured and marred, but it's not irreparable damage. The feelings of being undervalued, unappreciated, or that your life is purposeless do not have to be ones that you carry with you for the rest of your life."

I sipped my coffee while reflecting on my wall's sermon and remained perplexed for a moment. "You know, I thought I had already healed all that. I closed those wounds when I left him. I was able to walk with my head high again. I smiled and laughed without effort. I fell in love again."

"Yes,, your strength allowed you to love yourself through that time, but you were still broken. You were walking around castles in the sky, giddy and bewildered in liberation, enchanted by the freedom to love yourself enough to let someone else love you again even though you didn't feel like you deserved to be loved. You encountered a love that made you feel respect and connection instead of criticism and disregard, but you were still broken. Your morals never evaded you, your empathy for others remained constant, and even grew through it all, but you were still as broken as you are sipping that coffee right now. As time went on, the blinders came off, exposing you to your whimsical, narrow outlook as well as the wounds you thought you healed. Your own expectations fabricated from your desire to be truly loved & accepted ended up only hurting you more, as fanciful expectations generally do. You already knew that, but you were unconsciously taking measures to protect yourself and your heart from being wounded ever again. Yet through every gesture and endeavor, introspectively, your old fears and insecurities resurfaced, impairing your ability to see that they were damaging relationships with those you love and never being aware of it. The power of that knowledge is now crushing you, dismantling pieces all around you."

The tears were welling up now... seriously, how do I not run out of tears? I felt sick to my stomach.

"Go get the sledgehammer," the wall continued.

"What?" I replied.

"Go get the sledgehammer and knock me down," it said.

"Why would I do that?" I questioned.

"You're going to knock me down, but make sure you understand why you are knocking me down."

I did as I was told. My first blow was pretty weak, so I swung again. And again. And again. My swings got stronger. It felt amazing and I began yelling with every swing I took.

"I AM NOT A WHORE!
I AM NOT A DUMB BITCH!
MY PARENTS DID NOT DESERVE TO DIE.
I DO NOT DESERVE TO LIVE MY LIFE FEELING LIKE I SHOULD!"

I was so angry, I don't even know what came over me.

"I AM A GOOD MOTHER!
I AM THE ONE WHO RAISED THESE KIDS BY MYSELF WITHOUT YOU EVER DOING A THING!
I AM NOT WORTHLESS!

I AM JUST AS IMPORTANT AS EVERYONE ELSE IN THIS WORLD AND I HAVE A REASON FOR BEING!

I AM NOT USABLE AND YOU DO NOT HAVE CONTROL OVER ME ANYMORE!

I DID THE BEST I COULD WITH EVERYTHING UNTIL YOU KILLED ME!"

I fell to the floor in a heap of human shambles. No, no, no, I refuse to be a victim. I will not take on that title. I have life left to live and so much love left to give, but this disturbing force is so heavy and suffocating. How can an invisible fury like this cause so much mental anguish? Something completely unseen being powerful enough to transform every thought I think and every action I take… was incomprehensible to me. I turned to my wall for wisdom, but it was no longer there. As I sat among the debris, I remembered its last words to me…"but, make sure you understand whyyou are knocking me down".

I had to get my thoughts together. I knew what I was feeling, what I have been feeling. Isolation from the world while in a room full of people. Hopelessness… and an alarming disassociation from reality and self like I am existing in the world without actually living in it. Numb, empty, invisible. Bleak and unchanging.

NOTHING EVER GOES AWAY UNTIL IT TEACHES US WHAT WE NEED TO KNOW.

My art piece! It was not only inspiring, but it was also symbolic. I had to take back ownership of my thoughts and emotions to overcome this paralyzing unease. I had to accept the realization that no one else was going to completely heal my wounds and the only person who can truly help me, is me. All the anxiety, fear, and anger that has tornopen my soul to steal my core essence needed to be choked out.

I stood up and at my feet was a piece of rubble in the shape of a heart. I picked it up and placed it right on top of my new wooden block art that I rehung on the wall opposite me. My prison walls were gone. In a rare, but beautiful moment of clarity, I realized I was going to be ok. I had a lot to learn to get out of this awful place, positive affirmations to find, and healthy relationships to build with those who would encourage me and invigorate me. Yes, I had a lot to learn and it wasn't going to be easy, but it took my wall a lifetime to gain the wisdom it shared… and I have a lot of life left to live.

GRANDMA

BHUWAN THAPALIYA | NEPAL

She rose from her makeshift rustic bed
and strained her eyes in the morning sun
shining through termite eaten windows.
Drank a glass of basil water and then made
her way up a trail on a tough terrain
to the forest overlooking the Sunkoshi River
to collect fodder for her cattle.
An old kerosene lamp hangs in the window
of an abandoned building and carved wooden deities
flank a rickety gate. Poor eyesight, back permanently bent
from the burden of heavy loads, feet deformed
and ravaged by walking barefoot on rough terrain,
she looked older than her ancestral deity on a hilltop nearby.
Dry corn leaves rustled underfoot. She picked one
and rubbed it in her palms, smiling at herself
and kneeled down to quench her thirst from a
little burbling creek neighboring her path.
Thereafter, she hastened her pace humming
her favorite song, sung by her mother
when she was young.
"Plant a tree, then another, then many more.
Maybe we will be able to cleanse the world."

Every time when she hums this song,
she feels her mother humming it with her too.
Whistling, she walked deep inside the forest
and soon her doko was fully fodder crammed.
She looked at the deep blue sky and grinned
as a little girl with rhododendron flowers
in her hands high up in the Himalayas
and then sauntered slowly down the hill,
carrying heavy doko on her back with the namlo straps
on her forehead smiling at her neighbors
showing her uneven teeth, as they prepare
to spread animal fertilizer on their fields.
On the back of her polka-dotted cow,
there was a little bird.
The cows mooed loudly after seeing her.
She fed the cattle and then went inside the kitchen
to cook dal, bhat and tarkari.
In the adjoining room, her hungry children were
already getting ready for their school.

LIE FALLOW

JADE WALLACE | CANADA

When I wanted to know about tubal ligation, I turned to online magazines, which offered an impressive collection of horror stories. Grim tales populated by paternalistic gatekeepers wielding clipboards and impossible checklists. These articles were awkwardly prefaced by twee illustrations of bubblegum pink fallopian tubes, or stock photos of simpering nuclear families. Comments sections were equal parts sympathy and rage. According to these accounts, it was nearly impossible for a young, unmarried, childless person with a uterus to access permanent birth control, even in the ostensibly progressive era of the late 2010s.

But, being young, I was energetically stubborn, so I booked a day off work and left the city on a coach bus. When I arrived at my parents' rented house, I sheepishly asked my mother for a ride to my appointment, the purpose of which I demurely elided, and she kindly did not ask. We coasted past fields, some lined with fledgling stalks of corn, some thick with spring grass and grazing cows, some barren and gathering strength.

I spent another hour in the doctor's waiting room, skimming glossy magazines full of anachronistic recipes for strawberry chiffon pie. The appointment itself lasted ten minutes. "Have you thought about the pill? An IUD? Something temporary?" my doctor asked. For months, I'd read up on contraceptives: intrauterine devices, birth control pills, diaphragms, spermicidal gels, vaginal rings, cervical caps, hormone patches, condoms, internal condoms, progestin injections, ovulation calendars, the rhythm method. I'd read, too, about the erosion of healthcare coverage in the U.S. and how, even in my own province of Ontario, not all birth control is covered by our universal healthcare. The kinds covered, who can get them, and the extent to which they are subsidized, are subject to the government's regulatory whims. At the legal clinic where I worked, there was fresh evidence every day of the steady rise of low-wage, precarious employment. On the subway, ads announced the television debut of The Handmaid's Tale.

"I've thought about them," I said. "I'd prefer something permanent."

"Are you sure?" my doctor asked.

*

The summer after kindergarten, we went on a family camping trip. My grandmother asked me, Did you make any friends? One friend. Do you have a boyfriend? No. What good is a boyfriend? Do you want to get married someday? Maybe. As long as I can have four horses, two cats, two dogs, and a big farm. Do you want kids? Never. Then I'd have less time for the horses.

*

"I don't want hormones," I told my doctor. "I can't handle the mood swings." The last time I was on the pill I was doing my first Master's degree and spending several nights a week crying on my second boyfriend's kitchen floor. I didn't know whether to blame the pill, grad school, my boyfriend, or myself. When I finished school, moved to another city alone, went off the pill, and started dating women, the crying stopped as if I had turned off a tap. "And no insertions," I added. "I don't want to think about pregnancy ever again."

He nodded. "Doctors perform vasectomies for men every day. Women shouldn't be treated any differently."

Woman has never been the word I would pick. If pressed, I use agender or nonbinary. If no one asks, I don't volunteer. My gender has always been evasive. Regardless, I left my doctor's office feeling more understood that I'd expected, and pleasantly shocked by how easily I'd gotten a referral to a gynecologist.

At fourteen, I was a pious Catholic schoolgirl who failed to look the part. I wore oversized men's clothes, tucked my hair under my hat, and didn't know what to call myself. Tomboy made the girl who sat next to me stick gum in my hair. Every other girl in class had already begun to bleed. I had so far escaped that tide sweeping them toward adulthood, but I didn't feel left out. Secretly, I was relieved. Lying in bed at night, hands folded, I asked God to spare me. Fertility is a gift, I said. Give mine to someone who will use it.

When I found my underwear soaked red one morning, I still prayed. Let it be a hemorrhage. A fluke. The second time I bled, I gave up praying. I gave up God soon after.

*

While I waited to hear from the gynecologist, I talked to other people. My parents were unruffled, as though they had been expecting it.

"Your grandmother had a tubal ligation," my mother said. "At twenty-three. After your uncle was born."

"In the sixties? Didn't they give her a hard time?" I asked.

"Not that I heard."

My other older friends told me they had no problem getting tubal ligations decades ago; meanwhile my younger friends recounted exhausting searches for a compassionate physician. Why had it seemingly become harder to get a low-risk, highly effective procedure? Briefly, I wondered if medicine had somehow become more patriarchal. Then I realized the simple truth: my older friends, like my grandmother, had given birth before getting sterilized. My younger friends had not yet paid their debt.

*

On my friend X's seventeenth birthday, we walked to the grocery store with two other girls to get pop and a pregnancy test.

"Aren't you on birth control?" one girl asked X.

"Yeah, but I'm late this month," X replied.

"Would you keep it?" another girl asked.

"Maybe," X said. "My parents would be so pissed, but I don't know what they'd do." I knew what my father would do—he swore if I ever got pregnant, he'd kick me out of the house.

Later that day, we stood useless outside the bathroom door while X struggled. I wrung my hands, as though the possibility of an impending pregnancy sentence were mine. Finally, X came out smiling. I hoped my fate would never be foretold by such a lowly oracle. But all of ours would someday, one way or another.

*

Meeting the gynecologist required another day off work. I wore a suit so she wouldn't feel like she was offering life-changing surgery to the teenager I was occasionally mistaken for. In her office, I avoided the brochure "Storing Your Baby's Stem Cells," lest anyone think I was having latent maternal impulses.

A med student entered first, asking questions like whether my boyfriend could get a vasectomy so I wouldn't need a tubal ligation. No, I thought, because we might not last. Then the gynecologist came in.

"Have you considered other forms of birth control?" she asked.

"Yes, I've considered other forms of birth control," I said.

"An IUD?" she pressed.

"I'd really prefer something permanent."

"You never want to have children? Tubal ligations are technically reversible but the success rate is only seventy percent."

"Never."

"You'll need general anaesthesia. You could wake up with a colostomy if your bowel is punctured. Infection could set in up to three days after surgery. You could die."

"What's the chance of any of that happening?"

"Less than two percent."

"I understand."

"And you're sure?"

*

One night, my first boyfriend and I were taking the last bus from the university back to his house, folded into each other. The dim interior lights cast a blue haze over the glassy-eyed faces of the passengers.

"I'm not ready to have sex yet," I whispered suddenly.

"Oh. Well, that's okay," he said. "What do you need to be ready?"

"Birth control pills are not one hundred percent effective. I'm really terrified of getting pregnant." I did not mention that the prospect of an abortion terrified me, too. "I have condoms. Do you know how small the chances are of getting pregnant if we use both?"

"Yes. But the fact that there's a chance at all still worries me."

"We can use two condoms."

"That makes it less safe!"

"I know."

"I'm sorry."

"It's okay. We can still do other things, right?" he said.

I nodded, flooded with relief.

We dated for three years after that, and he never once acted resentful or tried to reform me. We're still friends now, in the way adults living in different cities generally are, speaking only a few times a year.

The night he and his wife had a baby, I was honoured to be among the first people he called, and I surprised myself with how happy I was for the three of them, even though, at the same time, I was as certain as ever that it was not a fate I wanted for myself.

*

I told my boss I needed a week off for surgery.

"Of course!" He said, looking concerned.

"I'll bring a doctor's note," I said.

"Don't worry about it!"

How lucky I was. To work for someone who was always kind to me, who offered me an all-too-rare, permanent position with paid sick leave. To have parents and doctors who accepted my convictions. To live in a province where the healthcare system covered the costs of the surgery, in an era when I didn't need any husband or guardian's permission.

*

One Friday night, my third boyfriend and I were walking down a quiet, residential side street with our arms around each other, making our way to an art show.

"I'm considering getting a tubal ligation," I declared, without segue.

"Oh. Isn't that permanent?"

"Yes."

"You're off the idea of an IUD?"

"Why get a new IUD every few years when I'm sure I never want children?"

"Not even with me?" he smiled that smile of plausible deniability I recognized from all the times he'd said we should get married.

"I like kids just fine when they belong to someone else. Do you want kids?"
"Maybe. Someday." He smiled again. "I bet our kids would be cute."

"I'm sure." I thought of my most recent pregnancy test—negative—and resolved never to mention it to him.

"I don't expect you to make a choice based on whether I want kids."

"I know. And I wouldn't." Still, it felt like I was slamming a door in the face of our would-be children.

*

Surgery was easy. I arrived early the morning of and spent my time in pre-op dozing. In the operating room, my gynecologist asked how I was feeling.

"And you're ready?" she asked. "And you're sure?"

"Absolutely," I said.

The anesthesiologist arrived to put me under. Anaesthesia ran like icy water into my vein. Is this how it's supposed to feel? I wondered, but was knocked out before I could ask. When I woke, I was alone again. Blearily, I whipped off my blanket. My abdomen looked more or less the same. No colostomy, no weeping cuts. Deep relief. My mother found me soon after. She drove me home late that evening, while I lay fully reclined in the passenger's seat, mesmerized by stars rushing past the top edge of the window.

*

My mother took care of me until my third boyfriend arrived the next afternoon. He stayed for days and cooked endless meals while I slept on the couch next to my cat who lay warm against my wounded abdomen.

Whenever I stood up, my boyfriend would say, What are you doing? I'll do it for you. I ran out of ways to say I love you and I'm so glad you're here and thank you. I wondered if I would ever have the chance to be as good to him as he was being to me. (I would not.)

Before week's end, I was healed enough to rejoin the living. I felt my gynecologist had fixed a decades-old, prenatal mistake by sealing up my fallopian tubes and sequestering my ovaries from the rest of my body. From the world.

*

When I was reading those harrowing online accounts of tubal ligation, I began to worry that all of us who wanted permanent birth control were doomed to wander forever in fruitless pursuit of our own autonomy. But none of us were wrong for believing we should have first and final say about our bodies. My doctors gave me an incomparable gift by allowing me to exercise that agency.

*

They were good doctors, but also perfectly ordinary. Any doctor could be just as liberating, if they aspired to it.

I have rewritten this account of my sterilization several times over six years, never wholly satisfied because I am trying to write for so many people at the same time. But I keep at it because this conversation is urgent. The U.S., which is a walkable distance from my home in Canada, is beset by regressive political efforts to reduce access to reproductive care including abortion.

I want my account to remind other people seeking permanent birth control that sometimes, in spite of all that stands in front of them, they will find it. They will find it even if they are unmarried, unassertive, childless, guileless, queer, meek, disabled, flailing, tender, timid.

I want to show bad doctors that some of us spend our entire lives completely sure of what we need. I want to thank good doctors for their remarkable ability to give us just that. I want my parents to know that they did everything exactly right.

I want everyone to see how easy it can be to hold one another up: cook for a loved one when they are sick; give an employee the benefit of the doubt; stand back and let someone become the person they long to be.

*

For years, I wondered how I could be happy about a surgery that has been a terror to so many. Like abortion, sterilization has been coerced or withheld as a means of control by states and medical systems. Used against people like me, and people oppressed in other ways, in an effort to convince us that our bodies are not our own. In 2021, Canada's Standing Senate Committee on Human Rights reported that sterilization is still forced upon Indigenous people, and that 'preliminary' evidence suggests people who are disabled, low-income, HIV-positive, Black, racialized, transgender, intersex, or institutionalized are also vulnerable to forced sterilization.

These days, I understand that permanent birth control is like sex: you do it in full awareness of how dreadful it would be if forced upon you. I'm lucky. I asked for my tubal ligation, would have begged for it, and it feels natural and right. The telos of decades of reproductive anxiety and gender dysphoria.

For five years now, I have been a bare field, and I am as satisfied as ever to carry only myself. My body is reserved for other forms of regeneration. I make art, tend gardens, dream of horses. A sole scar remains from the surgery: a small ridge on the smooth expanse above my fallow uterus. Sometimes, lying in bed at night, I run my fingers across the scar to remind myself that no lover, no lineage, no state, no mass of fetal cells, can claim this small space that is mine.

I SAW YOU

ZAYNAB ILIYASU BOBI | NIGERIA

The roads to happiness are broken.
The first step I made, I sprawled on the bodies of girls
whose voices have been singed by a flameless fire.
The Physiologist said, 60% of the body is water.
Let's say, a day of burning is equivalent to a litre.
How long until a woman exhausts her tears?
In my dream, I see the woman I am yet to become tossing
her body into the water. But when the fire comes, her voice
shrink into an echo whistling against the emptiness,
against the blooming void. What did you see before your voice
clutched onto silence? I asked. I saw water begging to be exiled
from the mouth of fire. I saw a woman holding ruin in her palms,
each line, pouring into a hologram of burnt memories. I saw another woman
learning the language of love from a lover with the smoothness of a mirage.
I saw a girl travelling through adulthood with purple skin.
What else did you see as the water hardened into a mirror? I asked.
I saw you.
Saw you.

You

MANIFESTO OF THE REPRESSED

ARATHI MENON | ENGLAND

We are not really sure we have the right to have this manifesto.
If we do, we hope it's okay to say what we want.

We intend to cause nobody any harm and we are sorry if it does.
We wonder how many rights can we have. Is there a number limit?

Some people think we are talking bullshit and they may be partially right.
The people who are partially right, insist they are fully right and we may agree with them.

We actually think
everything is fine and there is no need for this.

FREE

HARO ISTAMBOULIAN | USA & ARMENIA

Bombs are dropping like rain across the sea,
but here we are simply brushing our teeth.   We are not free.

Over here we shower but over there,
the rivers dirty water washes her feet.   I am not free.

You toast to life and love in a clear glass or three,
while drought dries their kidney,
as the government bathes in greed.   You are not free.

You wed your lover in the church's altar,
as the man stones and berates his daughter,
all without a simple show of grief.   She is not free.

Bailey, Peter, Kaley, Sawyer, thinking up names for
future lawyers but over there the country lets them be.
Their name will be their father's fathers,
all names without any honors and last names,
assigned from dictionaries.   He is not free.

And in thousands of years just as God is powerful,
the love He created has become so sorrowful,
but not to worry...   ...these are all things
                                                 you'll never have to see.

MEET THE GLOBAL AUTHORS

OF THE IHRAM'S 2023 LITERARY MAGAZINE

EWA GERALD ONYEBUCHI

...is an Igbo writer of short stories and poems. His works have been published in *Afritondo, Africanwriter, Bengaluru Review, Arts Lounge Magazine.*

LEILA ZAK

...a 16-year-old student in Hong Kong, passionately engages in writing and activism. Through her initiative, *Flowers for the Future*, she conducts monthly lessons and creative writing workshops for girls in Kabul, Afghanistan. As a self-published author, explores the Rohingya Refugee Crisis in her debut novel, reflecting the experiences of refugees she works with in Hong Kong.

BRITTANY DULSKI

...utilized her piece to bring attention to the women protesting since the Dirty War to find out what happened to their children who disappeared.

A. N. GRACE

...lives in Liverpool, England. His short fiction and poetry have appeared, or are forthcoming, in *Queen's Quarterly, The Racket, Menacing Hedge, Fantasy & Science Fiction*, and many others.

OLAYIOYE PAUL BAMIDELE

...is a writer, photographer, and student of mass communication. He's also an actor and a Christian. His works are forthcoming in *Spillword, Lunaris, Artlounge, Ice Floe, Ninshar Art, Kissin Dynamite, Kreative Diadem*, and elsewhere.

ELEANORE LEE

...a legislative analyst for the University of California, has a passion for fiction and poetry. Her acclaimed work, featured in journals like *Atlanta Review* and *Tampa Review*, includes winning the *2008 International Poetry Competition* and securing first place in the *November 2009 California State Poetry Society* contest.

NNEAMAKA ONOCHIE

...advocates on issues concerning women with plethora of emotions, experiences, opinions and information.

SHARON KENNEDY-NOLLE

...a Vassar College graduate, holds an MFA from the Writers' Workshop and a PhD in nineteenth-century American literature from the University of Iowa. She is the Poet Laureate of Sullivan County (2022-2024) and author of the chapbook *Black Wick: Selected Elegies*, chosen as the 2020 Editor's Pick by *Variant Literature Press*.

RUCHIKAA BHUYAN

...an 18-year-old student from Mumbai, currently attending Brown University, is a fervent human rights advocate who utilizes writing to champion causes such as LGBTQ+ rights, gender equality, and racial justice. Recognized nationally for her debut novel, *Until It Rains Again*, she also leads nonprofit initiatives like *Project Aafiyat* and *Girl Up Our Story*, striving to empower underprivileged women across India.

AMINA AKINOLA

...is a professional health personal and a product developer student at Google. She's a part-time writer and lover of arts. her works are published and forthcoming in *South Florida Journal, Lagos Maroko Print Issue, Brittle Paper, Nigeria News Direct Poetry Column, Visual Verses, Asterlit Magazine, Ice Floe,* and others. Her poems were shortlisted for the *African-Arise Contest 2020*. She is a member of the Hilltop Creative Art Foundation.

CLAIRE JOYSMITH

...born in Mexico, writes in both English and Spanish, often intertwining both. Central to her life and work is a passion for inter-cultural and inter-linguistic communication that promote more human understanding. An academic and teacher by trade, a translator by conviction, and a poet by urgent need, her work has appeared in magazines and anthologies across the Americas, and includes three volumes of poetry.

LENA PETROVIĆ

...a human rights lawyer and poet from Belgrade, Serbia, now residing in Washington D.C., previously offered legal aid to refugees in her hometown. Her poetry has been featured in Southeast European literary magazines, and her debut poetry book, *Sirens Don't Accept Cash* exploring themes of social justice, migration, and identity by published in 2023 by PPM Enklava publisher in Serbia.

TIMB SARA AUGUSTINE LAURENCE

...is the Cameroonian author of *LES CONFIDENCES D'UNE MUSE* (2021). Last year, the society of French poets awarded her the prize of the humanist poetry. At 23 years old, Sara is pursuing a PhD at the University of Yaoundé 1.

KASHVI RAMANI

...is the *IHRAM 2022 Creator of Justice Youth* award winner! She is s a *YoungArts* Finalist in Theater and Merit winner in Writing. She was *Arlington County's Youth Poet Laureate*, winning multiple Scholastic Writing awards, and her poetry has been featured in various publications, showcasing her active involvement in literary and poetry communities..

ADESIYAN OLUWAPELUMI

...is a Nigerian writer with a bizarre appetite for tomatoes. Winner of the *Cheshire White Ribbon Day Creative Competition 2022* & an Honourable Mention recipient in the *Starlit Winter Awards 2022*. his works have been featured in notable publications like *Poetry Wales, Konya Shamsrumi,* and *Brittle Paper,* showcasing his distinctive literary voice.

SURESWARI BAGH

...has a PhD in Odia Literature from Berhampur University. She teaches at Nalinidevi Women's College of Teacher Education in Bhubaneswar, India. Her poems are published in *Nissan, Janabadi, Katha,* and *Nabanita* among others. She serves as a member of the *Odisha Sahitya Akademi.*

PITAMBAR NAIK

...an advertising copywriter, moonlights as a poet and translator. His poetry and translations grace publications like *Ellipsis... The McNeese Review, and The Notre Dame Review.* Based in Bangalore, India, he authored *The Anatomy of Solitude* and *Fury Species,* and skillfully navigates between the realms of advertising and poetry.

SUSAN L. LIN

...is a Taiwanese American storyteller who hails from Southeast Texas and holds an MFA in Writing from California College of the Arts. Her novella *Goodbye to the Ocean* won the *2022 Etchings Press Novella Prize*, and her short prose and poetry have appeared in over fifty different publications.

HEC LAMPERT-BATES

...is a non-binary writer from Toronto, Ontario. Their stories can be found with *Fairlightbooks, Lit.202, Alternate Route Journal, Fleas on the Dog,* and others. They won the *2022 Bill Avner Creative Writing Award*. They are working on their debut novel.

GOODWELL KAIPA

...is a 27-year-old who lives in Monkeybay, Malawi. He loves writing especially poetry to understand the world around him. During his free time, he likes visiting the local library in his area to read a book or two..

HEATHER SALUTI

...is a visual artist, writer, expressive arts practitioner, and grief-worker. Their poems have appeared in *Canthius, Beyond the Veil Press, CV2* and others. They live with their partner and three cats Burt, Etta, and Babydoll on the unceded ancestral lands of the Musqueam, Squamish, & Tsleil-Waututh peoples or what is colonially known as Burnaby, British Columbia.

CYNDY MUSCATEL

...contributed to various publications such as *The Seattle Times* and *The Desert Sun*. Her works span fiction, non-fiction, and poetry, featured in journals like *The MacGuffin, Main Street Rag,* and *Existere*. The collection *Radio Days* is on Amazon and Barnes and Noble. Currently, she's crafting a memoir about teaching in 1960s inner-city Seattle.

ARINA ALAM

...is 29 year old transgender woman who lives in Gramsalika, a small village in West Bengal. Her family identified her as a boy when she was born and call her Kabir. She eventually became convinced that gender transition was absolutely necessary for her to achieve peace of mind.

ALYZA TAGUILASO

...is a Filipino General Surgery resident. Her poetry, recognized as a *Rhysling Award* finalist, has earned accolades in contests like the *Manchester Poetry Prize*. Published in *Electric Literature, Crazy Horse,* and more, her work reflects diverse themes, showcasing a notable presence in literary circles and earning shortlistings in prestigious competitions.

TYLER HEIN

...is a fiction and screenwriter from Edmonton, Alberta. He received an MFA in creative writing from the University of British Columbia. He received a 2017 *StoryHive* television grant and was shortlisted for the *2018 RBC/PEN Canada New Voices Award*. His first novel, *The End of the World,* is due for release.

SABAHAT ALI WANI

...is a writer, researcher and artist from Kashmir. Currently, she runs *Maaje Zevwe,* a feminist literary and cultural magazine of and about Kashmir, and aims to create a safe space for dissenting women's voices in her community.

NWUGURU CHIDIEBERE SULLIVAN

...is a speculative writer of Izzi, Abakaliki ancestry; a finalist for the *SPFA Rhysling Award,* a nominee for the *Forward Prize,* and a data science enthusiast. He was the winner of the *2021 Write About Now's Cookout Literary Prize.* He is published in *Strange Horizon, Nightmare Mag, Augur Mag, Filednotes Journal, Kernel Magazine, Mizna,* and elsewhere

ADESINA AJALA

...a 2022 Fellow of the Global Arts in Medicine (AiM), is a Cardiothoracic surgery enthusiast, training in post-grad surgical residency in Nigeria. He loves words. Their glitz, gleam & glories; fine & refined words blown from calloused hands & blistered lips. He is awarded the *Inaugural Freedom Voices Poetry Writing Prize (2019)* and *Ayamba LitCast Essay Contest (2021).*

MACKENZIE DUAN

...is a high schooler from the Bay Area who has been recognized by the *Alliance for Young Artists & Writers, Youngarts, Princeton University*, and *The Poetry Society*. Their work appears or is forthcoming in *Black Warrior Review, Frontier Poetry, Electric Literature, Sine Theta*, and elsewhere.

UZOMAH UGWU

...is a poet/writer, curator, and multi-disciplined artist. Her poetry, writing, and art have been featured internationally in various publications, galleries, and art spaces. She is a political, social, and cultural activist. Her core focus is on human rights, mental health, animal rights, and the rights of LGBTQIA persons. She is also the managing editor and founder of *Arte Realizzata*.

DAWN MACDONALD

...lives in Canada's Yukon Territory, where she was raised off the grid. Her poetry appears in journals ranging from *Asimov's Science Fiction* to *Vallum*, and has been nominated for a *Pushcart Prize*. Her first book, *Northerny*, is forthcoming from the University of Alberta Press.

ARYA F. JENKINS

...is a peace and justice social activist whose poetry has appeared in many journals and zines. Nominated for the *Pushcart Prize*, her poetry is widely anthologized. In 2021, her poem *Ruin* reached the finals for the *Derick Burleson Poetry Prize*. She has authored four chapbooks, a short story collection titled *Blue Songs in an Open Key* (Fomite Press, 2018), and a novel, *Punk Disco Bohemian* (NineStar Press, 2021).

TASNEEM HOSSAIN

...a Bangladeshi polymath, excels as a poet, op-ed columnist, fiction writer, translator, and trainer. Author of three poetry books and one on articles, her impactful works grace esteemed publications worldwide. A professional trainer and director of a prominent organization, she holds a Masters in English Language and Literature from Dhaka University, with four more books in progress

PURABI BHATTACHARYA

...is a full-time teacher and author. She is published with Writers Workshop India, she's released two poetry collections and has another forthcoming. Also a book reviewer for Muse India, her works grace *Livewire, And Other Poems*, and the *Yearbook of Indian Poetry in English 2021* anthology.

ROBERT PETTUS

...an English as a Second Language teacher at the University of Cincinnati, living with his wife, Mary, daughter, Rowan, and his pet rabbit, Achilles. Previously, he taught for four years, between rural Thailand and Moscow, Russia. His short stories have been published in numerous magazines, webzines, podcasts, and literary journals. His first novel, titled *Abry*, was published by Flick-It Books.

MIRA MOOKERJEE

...is a London-based writer, stuyding for her MA in Creative Writing at Brunel University. She has had work in published in *S/He Speaks: Voices of Women and Trans Folx* anthology, *Azeema Magazine*, and *The Journal of Fair Trade*, and was awarded the *Alison Morland Poetry Prize*.

AVE JEANNE VENTRESCA

...an American/Italian author, delves into social and environmental concerns across nine poetry chapbooks. Her award-winning verses, celebrated internationally, grace various magazines in print and online. With a notable editorial background, she edited for Black Bear Review and served as publisher for Black Bear Publications (USA) for two decades. Nominated for the *Pushcart Prize* in 2019, her poetry from the latest collection *Noticing The Colors of Ordinary* stands out.

DEBASISH MISHRA

...a Senior Research Fellow at the National Institute of Science Education and Research, HBNI, India, previously engaged with United Bank of India and Central University of Odisha, received the *2019 Bharat Award for Literature* and the *2017 Reuel International Best Upcoming Poet Prize*. His recent poems feature in various publications, and his book *Lost in Obscurity and Other Stories* was published by Book Street Publications, India (2022).

JOSHUA EFFIONG

...is a writer and digital artist from the Örö people of Nigeria. Author of a poetry chapbook *Autopsy of Things Left Unnamed* (2020). His works has been published or forthcoming in *580 split, Wrongdoing Magazine, Vast Literary Press, Native Skin* and elsewhere.

TANIA CHEN

...a Chinese-Mexican queer writer, features in anthologies like *Brave New Weird* and *Unfettered Hexes*. Published in various outlets, including *Strange Horizons* and *Pleiades Magazine*, they graduated from the Clarion West Novella Bootcamp in 2021 and received the *HWA's Dark Poetry Scholarship*. Tania currently serves as assistant editor at Uncanny Magazine.

OLIVER SMITH

...is inspired by Tristan Tzara, J G Ballard, and Max Ernst; his own work thrives on the poetry of chance encounters and the fusion of place, myth, and memory. Published in various outlets, his poetry has received two *Pushcart Prize* nominations, and he earned a Literary and Critical Studies PhD from the University of Gloucestershire in 2020.

BASUDEV SUNANI

...is an award-winning writer, veterinarian, and Deputy Commissioner, at the Ministry of Animal Husbandry. Some of his phenomenal volumes of poetry are *Asprushya, Karadi Haata, Chhi, Kaaliaa Ubaacha, Bodha Hue Bhala Paaibaa Mote Jana Nahin and Mu Achhi Boli*. He has also two novels, *Paada Podi,* and *Mashanee Sahara Delhi*. Apart from these, he has five volumes of critical essays.

DMT

...is a self-taught multidisciplinary artist, born in Pretoria, South Africa (1998). A poet and visual artist, DMT's work often draws from literary, sociological and metaphysical influences. They write from an autistic and non-binary perspective.

MEENAKSHI BHATT

...maintains a literary blog and expresses herself creatively through her writing. Her short story *My Garden* was published in Cornice Magazine. She has worked as part of the Carbon Almanac Network, a team of creatives and researchers that author Seth Godin created to prepare his latest almanac on environmental issues.

SAM SAFAVI-ABBASI

...is an Iranian/ American physician who left Iran over 35 years ago during the war between Iran and Iraq. He lived in Germany as a refugee for several decades. He then emigrated to the United States for medical school and medical training. He is practicing as a neurosurgeon in Arizona and is author of many scientific, medical articles as well as poetry, non-fiction and fiction essays. He works as a spiritual activist, physician, husband and father.

NNADI SAMUEL

...holds a B.A in English & literature from the University of Benin. Author of *Nature Knows a Little About Slave Trade* selected by Tate. N. Oquendo (Sundress Publication, 2023). A 3x *Best of the Net*, and 7x *Pushcart Prize* nominee. He won the *River Heron Editor's Prize 2022*, Bronze prize for the *Creative Future Writer's Award 2022*, and the *Virginia Tech Center for Refugee, Migrants & Displacement Studies Annual Award, 2023*

CHINEDU GOSPEL

...is a Nigerian poet, an ASSON student from College of Heath Sciences, Okofia. He is also a member of the Frontiers Collective. He enjoys playing chess and listening to music when he's not busy with school work or writing poetry. He recently won second place in the *Blurred Genre contest, 2023*.

ANANDA KUMAR

...is firm believer that the characters he creates are means to connect with the world around him. He lives day-to-day as a dentist in Chennai, India, writing in his downtime. His stories draw on the lives of the people who inspire him, His first published book, *Vanakkam Cosmos*, an anthology of novellas, was first released in 2017.

FADRIAN ADRIAN BARTLEY

...is Jamaican creative writer, his poems appeared in various online journals and magazines including *Pulsebeat* and *Gulmohur Quarterly*, Fadrian focus in writing is based upon life, nature, and personalities; his inspiration comes from within.

CHINECHEREM ENUJIOKE

... is an emerging black poet from Nigeria and undergraduate at Nnamdi Azikiwe University, studying Human Anatomy. Her works have appeared in *PoetrycolumnND* and *World Voices Magazine*. She is the Research Editor of The Moulder, a print magazine that publishes girl-child related issues in Nigeria.

ELAINE GAO

...is a rising senior at a high school in Oklahoma. Although English is her second language, she has always loved it more than her mother language. After reading almost 500 pages a day, she started to write short stories, poetry and even novels. She has just self-published her debut novel, *The Oracle*.

ALI ASHHAR

...is a poet, short story writer and columnist from Jaunpur, India. He is the author of the poetry collection, *Mirror of Emotions*. Following the release of his book, he was chosen as the *Best Debut Author for the year 2021* by The Indian Awaz and was the recipient of *India Prime 100 Authors Award*. His works have been published in 13 countries around the globe

KALI FOX-JIRGL

...is a professional content creator, writer, and published author who believes that writing is an art form and delights in the power of words. She specializes in capturing moments that transcend the page so readers can find connection and meaning within her work. It is her mission to spread knowledge, break the silence, and provide her readers with an elevating and inspirational reading experience one nugget of wisdom at a time

BHUWAN THAPALIYA

...is a poet from Kathmandu, Nepal. He works as an economist and is the author of four poetry collections. His poems have been published in various International Journals and anthologized in numerous books worldwide such as *Life in Quarantine: Witnessing Global Pandemic Initiative, IHRAM, Poetry, and Covid: A Project funded by the UK Arts and Humanities Research Council, University of Plymouth, and Nottingham Trent University,* among many others.

JADE WALLACE

...is a legal clinic worker, writer, book reviews editor for the literary arts magazine CAROUSEL, and co-founder of the collaborative writing entity MA|DE. Most recent works include Wallace's debut poetry collection, *Love Is A Place But You Cannot Live There* (Guernica Editions, 2023) and MA|DE's fourth chapbook, *Expression Follows Grim Harmony* (Jackpine Press, 2023).

ZAYNAB ILIYASU BOBI

...is a Nigerian-Hausa poet, digital artist, and photographer from Bobi. She is an undergraduate student of Medical Laboratory Science at Usmanu Danfodiyo University Sokoto, winner of the inaugural *Akachi Chukwuemeka Prize for Literature and Gimba Suleiman Hassan Gimba ESQ Poetry Prize 2022*, a *Pushcart Prize* and *Best of the Net* Nominee.

VYACHESLAV KONOVAL

...is a widely published and celebrated Ukrainian poet whose work is devoted to the most pressing social problems of our time, such as poverty, ecology, relations between the people and the government, and war.

ARATHI MENON

...an author and columnist in London, holds an MA in Creative Writing Prose Fiction from the University of East Anglia. Pan Macmillan, India published her memoir *Leaving Home With Half a Fridge* in 2015. Yali Books, an indie New York publisher, released her middle-grade mystery, *A Mystery at Lili Villa*, in 2021. Her awards and shortlisted awards include *Novel London* (3rd place), *UA 100X100*, *Penguin Write Now*, and *the Ivan Jurtiz prize* and *the BPA First Novel Award*.

HARO ISTAMBOULIAN

...is a writer and oil painter, focusing mainly on hyper-realistic portraiture and poems on taboo and human issues that the majority often try their best to avoid. Many open calls and juried poetry competitions have turned down Haro's work because these very real, daily issues are simply too grim for normal, public audiences.

International Human Rights Art Movement

The International Human Rights Art Movement (IHRAM) offers creative programs promoting freedom of expression, human rights, and social justice around the world. We envision a world where artist activism is honored as a human right, and a source of social change.

Visit *humanrightsartmovement.org* to see this change in action and browse our collection of groundbreaking anthologies, writing, fellowships and other programming.

Thank you for being part of a greater cause

Made in the USA
Columbia, SC
28 April 2025